To
Abiha ,

Best wishes

stay awesome!! ☺

Author of The Bee Hive

Thursday 5th March 2020

depetur ☺ x

Simon Adepetun was born in Whalley Range; Manchester in 1970 and has lived in Warrington, Cheshire since 1999. He has a 2:1 B.A (Hons) in English Studies and a Postgraduate certificate in Theatre Studies from the University of Manchester. Simon is married with three children, works as a Full time Sales Manager and enjoys spending quality time with his family.

Simon Adepetun

# THE BEE HIVE

AUSTIN MACAULEY
PUBLISHERS LTD.

A CIP catalogue record for this title is available from the British Library.

ISBN 9781786122209 (Paperback)
ISBN 9781786122216 (Hardback)
ISBN 9781786122223 (E-Book)

www.austinmacauley.com

First Published (2016)
Austin Macauley Publishers Ltd.
25 Canada Square
Canary Wharf
London
E14 5LQ

I dedicate this work to my precious gems, my shining stars whom I hold so close to my heart.

First and foremost I give God the glory for turning my dream into a reality, for the opportunity he has given me to pursue my passion for writing.

I thank my darling and amazing wife Abisola from the bottom of my heart. It has been a gruelling and sometimes arduous journey but we got there in the end. You have been so supportive every step of the way and never stopped believing in me.

To my children Benjamin, Daniel and Toni of which the inspiration to write The Bee Hive novel comes from. Especially to my daughter Toni for bringing her imaginative and creative mind into life and coming up with the novel's inspirational illustrations.

To members of my family for sharing in the excitement of this novel and for relentlessly egging me on.

I want to thank my publishers Austin Macauley and all the members of staff that worked tirelessly alongside me, investing so much energy into this venture so we could produce such excellent end product for your reading pleasure.

To all my colleagues at work, thanks for your continued support and encouragement.

Thank you all my treasured friends for your priceless advice, support, words of encouragement and love

For the good people of Warrington town (a small town with a big heart). Thanks for your continued love and support throughout this journey. Your invaluable support continues to overwhelm me. I hope I have done you all proud and may I continue to count on your unflinching support.

Finally for everyone else, too many to mention, that have had an input in the writing of this novel or encouraged me along the way, to my bloggers that have stuck with me on this long but rewarding journey.

I say thanks to you all.

# Contents

# Chapter One

## Meet the Family

My name is Daniel Chambers but you can call me Danny cos that's what my friends call me. To my teachers and parents well, I'm known as Daniel Jeremiah Chambers especially when I'm in trouble! I'm twelve years old, (almost anyway) and live with my mum, dad and two goldfish in a massive house. We have a big garden (the family's pride and joy) that's surrounded by a long and gigantic fence. It's great for barbeques but we live in England which makes any kind of good weather a luxury for us. This doesn't happen often so when it does, we take full advantage of it! You should see us in action, garden well groomed, deck chairs out, neighbours round, paddling pool out. We even make room for a certain someone's ancient surfing board (surfing in the garden?) Okay so that's going a little over the top and I understand that but I mean, do you blame us, you get the picture right? Talking about picture, I painted a really warm typical summers day in our house but I guess you're wondering why I never mentioned that word we kids love to hear...fun. Well to be honest, there isn't much of that around here these days, never was, never has been and there's a simple reason for it…P-A-R-E-N-T-S!

Now I would have thought being an only child and all that (aww I hear you say). Well thanks; it would have been nice to have had a sibling or two. However, I'm not quite sure that would have stopped me knowing what fun is really all about. I have loads of friends with b-o-r-i-n-g parents and no siblings but nevertheless, they tell me life is absolute whack! Maybe it's me that's the unlucky one! Having said that, I do have buckets of fun with my pet fishes. But I've always wanted to ask Mum and Dad why it never happened, why they never thought I'd love a sister or brother to call my own, to go with the goldfish but I never got around to doing it and it was not for want of not trying.

…Dad when am I going to have a brother? (Me at age 5).

(After a long silence)…Stop bothering me, ask your Mum.

…Mum, when am I going to have a sister? (Me now at age 9).

(An even longer period of silence) Dan, I'm busy, ask your Dad.

Well he said I should come and ask you…

Mum, Dad h-e-l-l-o someone, anyone, my request for a brother or sister or both (I'm now aged 10 and the silence, which is much longer than ever before is killing me)

So that was how my mum and dad answered my very simple question, and they say…parents know best!

(by the way I didn't die)

'Hello, ah Ian, can you make sure my entire schedule today goes ahead as planned, yes; Daniel, stop slurping your milk and use your spoon not your fingers to eat your cereal; Ian, are you still there? Good and make sure the jag is washed, dried, waxed, looking absolutely immaculate, smelling good and ready for action...'

## Bio Fact

Name: Philip Michael Chambers
Age: 42
Nickname: Dad
Hobbies: Work, work and more work
Most interesting fact: He loves telling me off!

*That's my Dad, never short of a word or two. He's an executive in a big company and has a very fancy car to show for it. A busy bee, but always has his eyes on me, watches me like a hawk!*

'Hi Jane, oh did you hear about Steve and Grace? They must be on an absolute packet to afford that kind of holiday especially this time of year. Tell me about it! Hold on a sec! Daniel Jeremiah Chambers, where's your school sweater?'

'Dunno.'

'Dunno, and what exactly does that mean?

*Like I really needed to explain that.*

'I only bought it the other day, a replacement for the replacement I replaced that apparently grew wings and flew away. You think money grows on trees don't you? Well I have shocking news, it doesn't so I suggest you go and find it,' she continued.

Daniel Jeremiah Chambers, don't do that, it's not nice, Daniel Jeremiah Chambers don't do this, you might hurt someone. Daniel Jeremiah Chambers don't talk with your mouth full, you could choke. Daniel Jeremiah Chambers, don't just barge in like that, show your manners. Yes, I had heard it all before and knew it was coming long before it came. That was a perk for living in this household and No this wasn't my voice, the voice of reasoning, you've guessed right; it was the voice of my Mum…

Bio Fact

Name: Susan Angelina Chambers

Age: 21!

Nickname: Mum

Hobbies: Shoppinggggggggg!

Most interesting fact: She is never wrong!

'Sorry about that, Jane. Are we meeting up for lunch on Saturday? Yeah spa and shopping sounds like a great combination to me. Janet! No way, tell me more…'

*Another busybody, now she never leaves the house without her special card, always up for saving a bob or two on me so she can get a few bits and bobs for herself! The way it works, Mum spends the money and it's all added to this well-designed card that Dad pays for. The internet (a very handy thing for our day and age) suggests it's called a credit card, Dad suggests it's a venture he regrets ever investing in! When I grow up, I'm going to be just like Dad owning lots and lots of credit cards so I too, can be rich just like him!*

'Honey, did I hear you invite Jane for shopping this Saturday?'

'Yes why?'

'Daniel's got football, remember, someone's got to take him.'

'Oh I totally forgot.'

'A bit of a giveaway Mum, Dad was waving at you, but you were both too busy gabbing on the mobiles,' I remarked

'Stop being cheeky to your Father and I Daniel.'

*Oh no, Mum's used the word Father and she only does that when I'm in trouble so I guess...*

'Why can't you take him Phil?'

'I'm going golfing with the lads remember, I've booked it for weeks.'

'And I can't cancel the date with Jane; you know what she's like. Well that settles it then—'

'Settles what!' I replied nonchalantly and with such speed that neither Mum nor Dad picked up on my sarcasm and rudeness all rolled in one.

'Your Aunty Katie will have to step in and take you.'

'K-a-t-i-e!' I shrieked.

'She's Auntie Katie to you,' she retorted.

'Oh come on Mum, you can do better than that! Katie, she's not even a relative,' I screamed my disapproval. She's your friend whom you insist I call Auntie,' I continued strongly.

'Watch your tone, Daniel, or you can kiss your birthday party goodbye and I mean it.'

'Dad!'

*I was looking for a sympathy vote from Dad but I should have known better!*

'I second that. Listen to your Mother, Dan, or there WILL be consequences!'

*While I pondered on what the consequences were likely to be, let me tell you a little bit about 'Auntie Katie.'*

### Bio Fact

Name: Katie Charlotte Jones

Age: unknown

Nickname: Auntie Katie (Very obvious)

Hobbies: She adores her pet cats

Most interesting fact: She treats me like one

For the record 'Auntie' Katie had known us way back and long before I was born. Apparently she had earned the right to the title of Auntie having always been there for us in times of trouble. Oh and helped us immensely by feeding me, changing my nappies when I was but a wee boy. Hence I was supposed to be eternally indebted to her. I take both my hands and wrap them around my neck with my tongue hanging loosely out of the corner of my mouth.

'Daniel, behave, Mum's right and I don't want to hear another word.'

'Oh come on, Dad, last time Katie, I mean Auntie Katie took me out it was to the Youth Club Summer Party. She missed a turn. We ended up gate crashing someone else's barbeque. It was embarrassing!'

'He's got a point you know.'

'Well if you have a better idea, Phil, let's hear it cos I'm not cancelling my shopping with the girls so it means...

'Your Mum's right, we all make mistakes, Daniel, even you.'

'Dad, that's where you're wrong, I AM an angel every time, all the time...'

Well, that's my family unless of course you want to actually meet our pet fish Perky and Rambo. They aren't talking goldfish but I guess it would really spook you out if you found out that they were!

So here you have it, a typical morning in our house...

'There you are you sneaky monkey. Where is it, Dan? Hand it over.'

'Hand what over? Whatever it is you're looking for, I haven't got it.'

'Aha! Mum, Dad, did you hear him? How do you know I'm looking for something?'

'You just said so yourself.'

'Dan, hand back whatever it is you took that belongs to your sister.'

Sister! Ah yes, O-K so I lied, I'm not an only child, well (sigh) meet my very annoying loud-mouthed sister Alice...

### Bio Fact

Name: Alice Olivia Chambers
Age: 10 going on 18!
Nickname: Pest

Hobbies: Combing her doll's hair till it goes bald

Most interesting fact: She was actually born to a family of Aliens!

Habit: Always making my business her business!


*I knew this quiet time would never last but I enjoyed every minute of it, something I would forever cherish in a long time...*


'Give it to me right this moment, Dan, and I mean it!'

'Dan!'

'I told you, Dad, I haven't got whatever it is she's looking for,' I repeated for the zillionth time.

'Mum!'

'Not now Alice, Your Dad and I are on the phone.'

'There she is.'

'There she is what?'

'Dangling out of your pocket, you liar, there she is and you said you didn't have her.'

Alice pointed her finger accusingly at me as if I was a piece of filth.

You better not have hurt her or else...

'...or else what? Here, take your stupid rag doll'

I threw the doll clumsily at Alice actually aiming for her head but she was well aware of this, dodged it and still managed to catch it safely.

'How many times do I have to tell you? She's a superstar doll and her name is Bessie.'

She caresses the doll quietly asking it if I handled her carefully and apologised to her for any maltreatment that I might have imposed on her. I felt like puking at the horrible sight.

'Who cares what her name is, and IT is only a doll.'

'You didn't have to throw her, you could have broken her you idiot.'

'Dad, Alice called me an idiot.'

'Dan, don't be so mean to your sister.'

'Me! She's the one that sits there combing that thing's hair all day long, that's all she ever does, it's annoying. Look, there's so much hair lying about in the house people will think we own a dog. I'm surprised the doll's not bald.'

I had pointed to the hair that was scattered all over the room but Mum and Dad didn't even blink. I guess they weren't interested at all in what I had to say, just what good old Alice did!

'You're just jealous.'

'Jealous of your big headed rag doll? You wish.'

'Mum, Daniel called Bessie a big head!' 'Look who's talking, toe rag!'

'Mum, Alice just called me a toe rag. I'm not!'

'You are!'

'Not!'

'Jealous.'

'Me, jealous of a matchstick doll with a dumpling for a head.'

'Mum, Dan called Bessie a dumpling head!'

'No I didn't.'

'Yes you did.'

'Didn't.'

'Did.'

The fact that Mum and Dad had hung up their phones and were now clasping their ears with both their hands suggested to me that Alice and I had succeeded in providing them the much needed early morning headache they were keen to avoid and to be honest, so was I.

'E-N-O-U-G-H!' Dad roared. 'School both of you, NOW!' he continued as he pointed to the front door as if we didn't know where it was.

'The Crofts are giving you a lift and they are waiting for you outside right now, so goodbye.' Mum added.

I wanted to ask if Mum had provided neatly cut cheese sandwiches in my lunch box today as yesterday's sandwiches seemed hastily prepared hence tasted yucky and ended in the belly of the unfortunate bird that I just happened to befriend during my break time. One look at Dad's now protruding eyeballs as he stood by the opened front door with our school bags in his hands waiting for us to make our exit so that he could wave us off suggested that I best keep my protest till later on, much later on!

'Give me that.'

I snatched Bessie and belted away.

'Dan, give her back.'

'Come and get her if you're worthy.'

'DAN! Mum, Dad. Toe rag!'

Alice was hot on my heels. Dad was left standing aghast by the front door where we had left him still holding our school bags. I turned round briefly as I ran and could see Mum through the window, both hands on her hips.

'No I'm not.'

'You are…

'Don't you dare throw her… DAN!'

…Now this really is a typical morning in OUR house!

Perky and Rambo

# Chapter Two

## The X-Periment

When it was bought to our attention that all Students were to converge in the School hall with immediate effect for a very important announcement, I speak on behalf of every single student in the School when I say we feared the worst. Could it be that despicable Mr Roughway, the deputy Principal was reversing his decision to retire at the end of the year and further heap more of life's misery on us? Or was it that the school was finally carrying out its threat to scrap the most delicious but very relevant Wednesday deluxe pizza day off the dinner menu to become a thing of the past and devastate us all? Maybe it was that for every time the School football team lost, each member would have to endure some sort of punishment, like walk the plank? We had lost that many times it was becoming a habit and the most worrying thing – I was part of that team. Or had History finally been identified as the School curriculum's weakest link, therefore to be removed with immediate effect, no questions asked and Mr Bonesworth, the History teacher relegated to the School kitchen! On a much lighter note, could it be that after what seemed like centuries since she'd been here, the lovely and angelic Mrs Steinway, the School Librarian would finally retire. My mind was bringing up all kinds of permutations and having started with what would be the good news then the not so good news, my mind was drifting backwards and forwards to the good and bad, it was at this point I noticed Mrs Coburn appear on the stage. Whatever it was, the answer was forthcoming, and this was much to the relief of us all.

What do you get when you cross a high school student with a Bunsen burner, a conical flask and laboratory? The answer, in our case, nothing unless of course you are Mrs Coburn the Science Teacher using an allegory to announce the school's annual scientist of the year award.

'This will be the biggest event of the entire calendar year and the most prestigious of its kind ever,' she would go on to add.

We nicknamed her Harry Potter for the way she moved her hands about like she was waving a wand!

'I'm looking for someone with innovation.'

Mrs Coburn spoke with quite a posh accent for a Science teacher. Rumour had it that she was actually born into a rich and very posh family and that generations and more generations before even that, meaning the family had loads of dosh. Her father was a Lord and mother a Lady. This therefore begged the massive question as to why she chose this boring life ahead of one where she would never lack any cash...I definitely know what I would have chosen! So here she is stuck with us in our boring school trying to make our boring lives exciting...

'Innovation? That rules you out,' I whispered to a mate.

'Someone with dedication,' she continued.

'Guess that rules you out, sucker,' my mate whispered back almost immediately.

'Young scientists, this year, I need you to set the science world alight!'

She was gesticulating like a sorcerer conjuring potion from a cauldron. The school definitely choose the right person for this!

'Besides the fame that we will bestow on our crowned Scientist of the year, in addition, he or she will win a mystery prize.'

'Wooooo!'

That was the sound of the whole school wooing. And when we all woo at the same time, it is quite loud!

'So without further ado, young scientists, let SOTY contest begin.'

SOTY or Scientist of the Year as it was commonly known. I guess the acronym could have been much worse. It was actually us kids that came up with the idea which the school tried so hard to get rid of, found that they couldn't and so decided to go with it, turned out to be a very wise decision.

Mrs Coburn threw both her hands high in the air. At this point I was expecting thunder and lightning to appear to really set the tone. To my bitter disappointment that didn't happen, so I had to make do with my imagination whilst popping the hundreds of balloons that failed to join the other hundreds now floating in the sky. All this effort to officially commence this year's competition.

After all the pomp and paltry, we knew it was time to swing into immediate action!

Just like Mrs Coburn had said, we needed an idea full of innovation, we needed to be fully dedicated to the cause and I knew exactly how to do it!

Mrs Coburn

# Chapter Three

## The Slime!

We are the Slime
We're going home to you
We are the Slime
What ya gonna do
Sing it from the rooftops
Sing it on the streets
Sing it in the bathroom
Sing it when you eat
Drum it in their ear holes
Drum it to your friends
Sing it to your Parents
May it never end?
Slime! Slime! Slime!

I used improvised drums made from empty cans of paint that I found in Dad's shed and with Mum's wooden spoons for drumsticks, the beat was well and truly on. I loved music from the band The Slimes, they were my favourite, but in our household, to say it wasn't everyone's cup of tea wasn't too far from the truth…

Alice stormed straight into my room with her hands covering her ears. She had her annoying doll with her. I should have guessed what Alice was suggesting by her mere action and ill-timed mime but since she looked very uncomfortable and I was enjoying it, I jumped at the opportunity to further wind her up by ignoring her.

'Turn the music down!' she screamed.

'Pardon?' I shouted back.

'Will you turn that horrible racket down?'

'I still can't hear you, I shouted back (even though I heard her enough to respond to her nonsense demands, but clearly choose not to).

'DAD…'

The moment Alice bellowed out 'Dad'; the wax that was stuck in my ears miraculously disappeared. I was now able to hear her and respond promptly by turning the music down just a little.

'Mum and Dad have been screaming their guts out from downstairs for you to turn the crazy music down.'

'I didn't hear them.'

'Obviously, as you were too preoccupied making such a terrible din!'

'Whatever! Anyway can't you read? Did you not see the 'KNOCK BEFORE YOU ENTER sign on my door next to the 'KEEP OUT' sign?'

'No.'

'They weren't written in giant bold letters for nothing now were they? What do you want?'

'Are those Mum's wooden spoons you're using for drumsticks?'

Alice pointed to them as if they were an abomination.

'And what if they are?'

I declared without a care in the world. I seemed prepared to give the worst as well as receive it.

'And are those cans of paint from Dad's shed?'

'The cans are as empty as your head Alice, can't you tell?'

Alice was fuming. I don't think she liked being called an empty head but seriously she had it coming. She was turning bright red and threatened to explode any second now. This was definitely the fun part and I was loving every minute of it!

'What do you want, Alice? I'm very busy as you can see.'

She then did the most ridiculous thing and started to sniff around the room like a dog in search of a bone.

'Alice! What do you want in my room?'

'Hmm, what's that smell?'

Alice was stood rooted to the spot with her nose stuck in the air sniffing a corner of my room as if she were a rabbit. She was violating my private space and I didn't like it one bit.

'What smell?'

'That rotten egg smell.'

'Oh that smell, have a guess,' I laughed cynically.

'Urgh! That's disgusting.'

Alice pressed two of her fingers hard against her nose to repel the smell. The look on her face suggested that it didn't work.

'That's what happens when you barge into my room uninvited, it's the reason you have your bedroom and I have mine so remember that next time – now get out!'

Alice was in a world of her own. She was trying to say something but was suggesting that the smell in the room wasn't enabling her to do so, her acting was so lousy. I stood there staring at her. I wasn't trying to guess what she was meaning to say, I was thinking of what to do to that silly doll of hers once I had my hands on it. My thoughts somehow found its way out of my mouth.

'One day I'm going to take your glamour doll…'

'I've told you time and time again, she's a superstar doll Alice declared.'

'…and I will pop its head off and dump it in the bin.'

'No you won't.'

'Yes I will.'

'Then I will take your stupid slimy CD collection…'

'They're called the Slimes.'

'…and I will smash them to bits.'

What did I just hear Alice say! Did I actually hear her correctly? Did she really say that she would take my priceless all time Slime CD collection and smash it to bits? She had better not. Alice was smirking so I guess I wasn't just hearing things then. Now she was really out of order for that, absolutely. She would dare to even dream of manhandling the precious and most sacred item in my room, in fact, in the entire house! The most valuable piece of possession that I have in life! Was Alice totally insane for even thinking of saying what she just said! She must be. To dare talk in this abominable way and even utter such filth about the biggest pop band on the planet, a band parallel only to the likes of the legendary Beatles. Oh yeah, only someone totally insane could talk this way about the Slimes and attempt to even think of getting away with it. Prior to this, a line had been drawn and this very day, Alice had definitely gone cuckoo in the head, and in no mean terms, had crossed that line!

'You wouldn't dare,' I threatened as soon as I recovered from the initial shock and then somehow managed to get my thoughts together.

'Oh yes I will.'

Alice grabbed my Slime greatest hits collection CD that was on my side table. My heart skipped a beat as she did. She waved it in front of my face a couple of times as I tried to scoop it off her whilst avoiding the urge to just faint! I wasn't enjoying this one little bit because the CD wasn't in its case and the high risk of it getting scratched was just unthinkable. Why oh why was Alice doing this to me?

'Alice, don't do anything silly, give me my CD.'

'Take back everything you said about poor Bessie and tell her you're sorry.'

'What!'

As if I'd be caught dead apologising to a piece of rubber and thread!

'You're obviously not deaf. You heard what I just said,' Alice retorted.

'YOU take everything YOU just said back,' I demanded.

'Absolutely not,' Alice yelled back.

'Really, CD NOW.'

'APOLOGY NOW or say goodbye to your stupid CD. What will it be?'

I looked on in horror staring at my invaluable asset in the evil Alice's grasp. I really didn't want her to scratch it as that would be my life completely game over, and by the look of her horrible long, crusty finger nails, there was a very high chance that she could.

'Alice, I'm warning you.'

'Now you want to threaten me do you?'

'Pack it in you two upstairs will ya? I can't hear myself think with all your shouting.'

'Mum, Alice won't leave me alone,' I shouted back.

Alice turned away to respond to Mum. Only owls had the ability to turn their heads all the way round 360 degrees and maintain their balance and since Alice wasn't an owl, no sooner had she turned, I snatched back what rightfully belonged to me and with it went the need for any apology!

'You think you're clever.'

Well obviously, I had my CD back and she didn't get any apology so yeah I think I'm very clever!

'I was going to say that tea's ready but something tells me you're already full,' Alice continued.

'I'll be down in a second now get out.'

I placed my CD carefully in its case and then put it in my special box that was in my cupboard, something that I should have done earlier. It was special because it was made of indestructible metal and it came with three different combination codes making it virtually impossible for any menace to have access to. I guess the creator of this special box must have had the likes of Alice in mind. With my sister still cowering over my shoulder I swiftly administered the three codes then pointed to the door.

'With all pleasure,' she replied and waltzed off.

Alice, in my eyes was taking too long to exit my room; a surprise considering her displeasure at entering it in the first place. I needed to help her along the way which I did with a quick but firm shove that saw her fly out of my room. I heard Alice scream and this was soon followed by the sound of her rolling clumsily down the stairs and eventually clattering into several objects. It was probably Alice up to her old tricks again and I wasn't going to be fooled. I slammed the door behind her bidding good riddance to bad rubbish. With Alice finally out of my room and sight, I quickly produced a big jar containing a thick green slimy jelly substance, the real reason for the reeking smell. Between you and me, I had been conjuring up this experiment for weeks with the hope of winning the school's scientist of the year award. I had been working at it all day; I needed to create a distraction for all the noise I would make hence the loud music, my improvised drum beating was just further cover up along the way. If Mum and Dad had wind of what I was up to; my experiment would have been destined for one place and one place only, the bin!

I had slyly thrown into a conversation I had with Mum and Dad a few days ago about how nice it would be if I was to win the scientist of the year award. We all agreed. How nice it would be to win the 'mystery prize' which would go a long way in showing how responsible I could be. We all agreed, and how nice also it would be if I was able to use my bedroom for a lab to fit the purpose. Mum and Dad totally disagreed! Mum complained in advance of how her beautiful house would become a pitiful sight and trusted that I wouldn't dare attempt it. Dad complained about how much it would cost him to put things right for fear of the earache he'd get from Mum and they went on and on and on and on…

The end product of my day's hard work was the contents of the jar that I was proudly holding and yes I was very proud because despite the entire odds stacked up against me, I had done it. I had succeeded. I had not succumbed to the pressure of failure to those who would say you won't do it because you can't. I was like the great inventor of the telephone Alexander Bell that we learnt about in Mr Bonesworth's class.

'In the eyes of the public he was the stupid one, the silly one, the insane one, the hopeless and useless one until he invented the telephone which would change the world forever!'

Yes, I had succeeded where many had failed and this was for the zillions of people all over the world that had tried hard to succeed but failed.

'This,' I screamed at the top of my voice, 'this is for you all!'

I held my end product aloft high above my head as if it was a trophy. I was happy to continue to celebrate my victory but for the interruption via my phone that started to ring. I had the latest Slime single as my ring tone. I produced my mobile phone, last year's present from Santa.

'Yeah, whassup?'

'What do you mean am I sure the ingredients are correct? Of course they are, you gave me the list remember? Why, what's the problem? What do you mean it looks nothing like volcano lava to you? Yes, it does stink like your fart actually and it's definitely green in colour, different like we agreed.'

'Daniel! Tea is ready and it's getting cold,' Mum bellowed.

'You're wasting your time, Mum, he's deaf!' I could clearly hear the little rotter Alice remark along with her horrible gut wrenching giggle.

'I'm coming,' I screamed trying to hide my rage.

'Great, now you tell me. Look I've got to go Ben, tea's ready. I'll sort it out later when the coast is clear bye.'

Why in this world did we ever come up with the crazy idea of inventing the phone in the first place, especially the mobile phone? Because if we didn't have it I would not have just been informed that one ingredient was missing in the experiment and this explains the raucous smell and foul looking coloured specimen. It was also suggested that in the best interest of winning the scientist of the year award, I would need to accept that the days spent toiling away at this venture was a total waste of my precious time and to start all over again hence my burning rage. My supposed momentous day turned sour and it didn't end there as in my haste to hide my experiment in a safe place (my wardrobe) before Mum or anyone else for that matter made an unexpected guest appearance, I tripped and the contents poured all over my clothes including my Sunday best.

Getting downstairs to have cold tea was the least of my worries right now as I was staring at my completely ruined Sunday best and all my blood and sweat invested over my project was in vain, the now empty glass jar before me confirmed this. Oh and just for the record, the ring tone on my phone is titled- Disaster, something that I was clearly not too far from. Oh the things I would do to Alice for this, just she wait and see!

Slime 'Greatest Hits' CD

# Chapter Four

## The Bee Hive

One thing I derived a lot of pride from was the fact that I was a Jack of all trades and master of none. I was in my school team for virtually everything: football, chess, cross country running, cricket, swimming, you name it, and I did it all! Don't get me wrong, I know you'd be tempted to think that my school was a good for nothing community shack, too small to provide enough numbers for any kind of sport without the likes of me popping up here there and everywhere, don't think that because you're wrong. Talent, that's what it was, my rare untapped talent oozing out for all to see.

My Dad would argue that he'd have to lay claim for this and how I have him to thank for such avenue that would lead to fame and fortune. He would sit me down and spend hours revisiting his heyday, and I repeat heyday, stories of how he was the best athlete around and if not for certain elements beyond his or anyone else's control, he would not have missed the 'boat' and would have been very famous in the world of athletics. I would in turn sit with him for hours, with no choice in the matter listening reluctantly as he spilled out the story of his life. He would always take it upon himself to remind me of what he could have achieved those many years ago if only he had listened to his heart and not his head! Granddad Chambers would have a completely different opinion of things and who was I to take anything Granddad would tell me seriously anyway!

So on this eventful day, I use the term eventful very loosely indeed as it would be a day that would stay in our young memories for a very long time however for the very wrong reasons!

We had just trudged off the pitch after the blast from the referee's whistle signalling the end of the football match. It couldn't have come soon enough for us as we endured an absolute trouncing from the boys of the local Grammar school. Our record for the current football season was far from impressive. I mean there was always going to be the victor and the vanquished. We had vanquished that many games of recent we lost count, victorious in very few games that we could count! On this occasion the team coach used the words abysmal and disgraceful in one sentence, something he hadn't done in a long while. Our performance was so bad that most of the school and parents watching had left by half-time. Even the School's bus driver who volunteered to drive us all home at the end of the match and had stayed behind in his own time suddenly remembered he had to be somewhere urgently and hastily left. This meant we would all have to walk home unless we had a plan B which I didn't have!

So with coach clearly unimpressed, he didn't mince his words when he demanded to know from us what it was that went so horribly wrong.

## Bio Fact

Name: Jeffery Edward Miles
Age: 51
Nickname: Coach
Hobbies: Keeping the whole school fit
Most Interesting fact: He was an ex-professional
footballer

The coach's real name – Mr Miles, but mark my word you didn't want to call him that. Well not for the sake of a lap or two around the school football pitch anyway, (and trust me it was a big pitch) so for us, he was simply known as coach. Coach by nature, coach by name. So back to how the coach was feeling after our latest drubbing, shell shocked wasn't the word. I mean, this was a man who had coached famous football clubs to greatness. Your Arsenals, your City's and even my beloved United. Surely coaching a bunch of kids would be a breeze in the park for him! Well, now he was going right back to basics, he wanted answers and he wanted them quickly. This was an avenue for us boys to come clean, reflect on such a recklessly poor performance, acknowledge our shortcomings as a stepping stone to greater things using the best medium know to the human race…silence. Someone however forgot to tell me that! Surely there was no one among us born with the audacity to confront this great man? So what followed next was something straight from the world of the extra, extra ordinary. Dumbfounded, baffled, gob smacked, surprised, confused maybe, take your pick of the words to describe the situation once I dared to open my mouth.

It was something colossal neither coach nor the rest of the boys had bargained for. Without mincing words I told him how very disappointed I was, too. At this point one of coach's ears started to twitch, I didn't see it – the rest of the boys did. I confidently went on to add that we had a much better chance of beating the School girls' football team than our opponents if they continued to be bigger and stronger than us. One of the boys, Ben (the same Ben I spoke to over the phone the other day) quickly agreed with me.

## Bio Fact

Name: Benjamin Alfred Jones.

Age: 11.

Nickname: Benji.

Hobbies: Being my best friend for life.

Most interesting fact: He has an unlimited supply of farts.

Coach's jaw hit the ground almost immediately. As a matter of fact if it had hit the ground any harder, we would have witnessed an earthquake! He cracked his knuckles hard something he did on the pitch sideline especially when we were losing, we'd seen him do it so many times. This time it was so loud it sounded like a fire cracker had gone off! I could feel several eyeballs pop out of heads, suddenly glued to my face. The boys were all holding their breath; tongues were hanging loosely at the corner of their mouths awaiting the full impact of what I had just dared to say to be digested.

It was clearly my I-wish-the-ground-would-open-up-and-swallow-me-moment but it didn't happen like it never ever happens when you want it to.

For those who hadn't held their breath, they soon had good reason to do so as someone let off a silent but deadly fart and it stunk, talk about choosing the right moment, and we all knew who it was, at least I did anyway. Once my eagerness to share my observation with a coach of such high standings worthy of his thirty odd years' experience had finally subsided along with the very disturbing foul smell, he gleefully suggested since I knew best that I stayed behind after school and help him re-organise all the equipment in the gym. The privilege came along with a phone call to my Parents advising them of my latest demeanour. I would have willingly declined the offer but was given no choice in the matter!

Ben, who was my bestest friend ever since we were both toddlers so the story goes, he obviously didn't want me to face the punishment alone and for his loyalty, he would be assisting me with the added privilege of a call to HIS parents informing them of his act of treachery! It didn't occur to me that maybe if we were as equally strong and fast as our opponents we'd have half a chance. Well it did two hours after school later!

A phone call to my parents was just something I could ill afford right now especially with my twelve birthday perilously around the corner! I would have a celebration never to forget in a long while but that would come later on. For the moment, I had to endure the embarrassment of staying after School and serving my punishment and even the company of my best friend did little to soothe the pain! Something told me I should have done like all the other lads, kept my mouth firmly shut! And just for the record, we had already in fact played the girls team and LOST!

It was the longest two hours of my entire life and after what I had been through; I couldn't leave the school premises fast enough. I just wanted to go home, face the music then get some well-deserved rest… Benji, on the other hand, had ideas of his own!

'Come with me, I want to show you something.'

'Benji, do I seriously look to you like someone who wants to see anything other than my bed right now?'

'You have got to see this.'

'What?' I eagerly enquired.
'Come on, you're going to love it.'

'Benji you say this all the time and when we get to what it is you want to show me, I discover it's not worth the effort and a mere waste of my precious time.'

'This is different.'

'Just tell me what it is, whatever you say, I'll believe you,' I muttered.

'Seriously you have to see it to believe it you'll love it, c'mon.'

I remember those were the exact words Mum said to me about high school, 'You'll love it,' she said. I so stand to be corrected to this very day! So when Ben ushered me on and I literally dragged myself along like someone in lead boots, unsure of what to expect, (and I had clearly earned every right to be mind you) once again the ability to say 'No' was deserting me.

'C'mon it's a surprise,' he added gleefully.
Well, if the surprise was in the shape of a nice warm foamy bath to soothe my aching bones followed by a

cosy bed, then I was all in, (I had this funny feeling that it wasn't) however if it was anything like the 'surprise' awaiting me at home, then one was more than enough for the day thank you very much. I had already wasted two hours of my life which I was never ever going to claw back.

'Oh stop being a sissy, it's only a five minute walk off the footpath and besides, it's on our way home anyway so…'

Benji cut short his conversation and trotted off convinced I was right behind him. I had lived to trust him all my living life and he had never let me down so I speedily asked myself a million questions all starting with the word 'why' as I followed him like a dog in search of a lost bone. We walked through the park, over the bridge, through the marshes, past the stream and through the fields. 20 minutes later we arrived at a derelict looking hut…

'Here we are,' Ben pointed proudly at the wooden shack as if it say 'I told you won't regret coming.'

Oh how he was wrong!

'Well, what do you think?'

'What do I think? I'm lost for words right now.'

Seriously I'm not kidding plus I was unsure whether he wanted a long version of my thoughts or a very short one! Benji on the other hand well he was chuffed to bits. Notice I used the word HE!

'It's a hut.'

Well I knew what a hut looked like but this did not match my description at all.

'What on earth …?' I was clearly lost for words as I stared at the despicable sight before my eyes.

'Welcome to home sweet home.'

I was completely shattered and didn't even have the energy to point at it. But for the record, a phrase I so love to use, the hut was an absolute bomb site! It was two; possibly three different shades of colours, it was in a rotting state of decay with chunks of wood already dropping off its sides. The roof appeared to have several holes scattered about in it. I noticed one hole bulging with nylon was so badly patched it looked like a nest had been stuffed in it to possibly stop leaks from within. It was embellished with cobwebs near the door's entrance and corners like they were its trademark. It was in a most pitiful state. Home sweet home! It was more like welcome to ghostville to me.

'Well, don't just stand there. Feel at home, take a look inside. C'mon.'

Was it really necessary, I mean if this was what it looked like from the outside, I dreaded to imagine what it would look like from the inside! Regardless of my thoughts which clearly didn't matter, when Benji eventually opened the creaking door that threatened to completely drop off any moment I expected a colony of bats to fly out and rats to scurry through the door but that surprisingly didn't happen. He flung the door wide open and ushered me in. I reluctantly obliged insisting that he take the lead. Benji being that kind hearted and thoughtful friend shoved me inside, no questions asked!

'How about this then?'

'Excellent, much better than outside for sure considering that I can't actually see a thing, it's pitch black!' I remarked.

Oh yeah I forgot, hold on, all will be revealed.

Now I was really pushing my luck as it just dawned on me why he insisted on taking a torch with him. He produced it from his pocket and switched it on. He flashed the thin beam of light about but before you could say Jack Robinson the batteries had run out and we were back into the comfort of darkness again. I don't know about him but my heart was beating awkwardly pounding against my chest threatening to pop.

I could now just about make out Benji walking around arms stretched in front of him as he went along, he was still searching for something. I simply concentrated on following his every move. He stopped suddenly, felt about again then shrieked in delight.

'Here it is, and then there was light.'

No sooner had he uttered those words the place was illuminated and that 'it' was revealed as a very rusty ancient-looking oil lamp so old I was amazed it was still working.

'Ben, this mucky, smelly, old hut that you seem proud of, it's a first class mess,' I remarked as I pegged my nose down with two of my fingers. I mean it's dusty, dirty and a host of other things.

I wiped my hands across the table and took with me a generous handful of dust and dirt.

'It's not that bad.'

'It's not that bad? What planet are you on? H-e-l-l-o! Look down at the floor, there are several wooden planks missing, the rest are rotting away.'

He seemed very surprised at my candid opinion. I on the other hand wondered why.

'Yeah I admit this place needs some tender loving care?'

What?!

'This mucky, old, smelly, dusty hut or as you call it first class MESS actually used to be a bee hive many, many years ago.'

'Yeah question is how many years ago are we talking about?

I swiped a cobweb with my hand from the side of my face that I had walked into and wiped it against my trousers in disgust.

'A couple.'

Anyway, how do you know what it used to be?'
'I searched it on the internet.'

'Great, you might want to search for your local Ghostbusters too, see ya, bye.'

'Wait, where you going?'

'I am going home Benji, I do actually have one you know.'

'OK, but hold on, think about it, remember what your Mum and Dad told you?'

I shook my head because frankly I couldn't, they had told me so much.

'What about?'

I tried to lighten up the situation to somehow compensate me for all my precious time I had wasted on this most pointless journey, I sensed that I had failed miserably trying to achieve either!

'Well you know your parents and how they constantly complain about the state of your bedroom when you carry out your experiments, you said so yourself, yeah? How your dad would say 'can't you take your experiments elsewhere?'

He tried to mimic the way Dad talked but he wasn't even funny I just wanted to go home. I barked out a reluctant 'yeah' in response anything to get out of this place and on the path to freedom – home!

'They go on about how messy your room is, and to be frank they do have a point yeah? I mean just the other day your mum referred to it as a tip yeah.'

'Yeah, okay get to the point.'

I was getting tired of playing the yeah game, whatever it was Benji wanted to say, I just wished he would spit it out. I have learnt in the past that a conversation with too many yeahs never ends well!

'The point I'm trying to make is if we want to be serious scientists, serious enough to win the school science award, we need a place away from distractions, a place where we can do what we need to do.

Yeah, we needed a place away from distractions and not with distractions. I mean it was a massive understatement to say the place was a mess! At this point I left Benji to ask and also answer his own millions of questions.

'So here's the idea, we clean this place up, brighten it up, make it our own.'

'You are joking aren't you?'

Now it was Benji's time to shake his head.

'What are you talking about? This is mission absolutely impossible. Look around you, tell me what you see. Honestly have you not seen the state of this place?'

I eyeballed the whole room for what it was worth, it was horrible. I had just that moment noticed the windows that weren't broken were so covered in black muck no wonder it was so dark inside.

'We move our stuff here, create our own mini lab, have our own space, peace and quiet, what do you say to that?'

After dragging me all the way down here and having gone through the pain of the many yeahs, I felt I was owed a concrete explanation as to why and sensed an apology was well and truly in order. It wouldn't go all the way as to compensate for sheer waste of my precious time but would be a good start. I mean, was it actually worth the journey all the way here for this all for what Benji had in mind, a wacky idea. Did he really and truly want me to answer the question?

'Listen to yourself. Look, why don't we just leave and go home, I've had enough for one day, what do YOU say to that?'

'Dan.'

'This hut is in the middle of nowhere,' I interjected when I had finally digested the magnitude of Benji's all-time mess.

'No it's not, there is life all around us you know.'

He brushed the tattered curtains to one side with a single swipe.

'Look through this, how about that?'

'What is it I'm actually looking at?'

I quizzed Benji as when he said THAT, I presumed he was talking about the state of the window caked in so much fifth from cobwebs, bird droppings and squashed insects of which I could barely see out of. And eventually when I did, a few stray cats chasing birds about was as much signs of life as I could spot.

'What don't you see? I'll gladly tell. You don't see nagging parents, pesky sisters and in my case brothers. Shhh, listen to that.'

'What, I can't hear anything.'

'Exactly, just peace, quiet and an opportunity to make something big, great, beyond our very own imagination. Something we have both been yearning for and haven't enjoyed in a long while, so what do you say?'

'This place, but it's not ours, what if the owner comes and catches us in here. Then we'll be in real trouble something I can ill afford right now.'

'No one's going to catch us in here; told you it's not been used for years. Look, you are my bestest friend in the world and what do best friends do?'

'They look out for each other.'

'Exactly.'

'But look at this place, it's a total wreck.'

'Well like I said, there's nothing a good old scrub here and there can't do, boy power!'

That was the point in our conversation Ben would clench one of his fists and thrust it at me and I would in return meet my fist with his touching it faintly, it was our signature moment.

'How about people passing by.'

'We will have little trouble with that, come here, let me show you this.'

Ben led me outside and pointed to a sign that I hadn't noticed earlier. It read the following-


**Warning!**
**Any introoder trespassing this proparty will be exterminated**
**You have been warned!**

This was clearly Benji's proud moment and I didn't want to ruin it by pointing out the spelling errors and the fact that the word 'exterminate' was used exclusively for Daleks. These words could be easily and discreetly amended if I was to buy into this whole idea. Convincing Mum and Dad that experimenting in my bedroom was indeed a good idea a much more difficult preposition. So, I quickly changed my shaking head to a nodding one.

'Yeah there's a bit of work to do here I agree but if anyone can, we can,' Benji retorted.

Bit of work! That was the understatement of the year!

'Well, no one has been here ever since so it definitely works. So what's it going to be, disturbing parents and the distractions of pesky siblings or our own space where we are Kings and we rule?'

The last part of his speech sold the idea to me. All I needed to do now was devise a way of getting all my equipment out of the house and into the new abode without arousing suspicion. I thought about it and I knew just how. I shook Ben's hand that had been left hanging in the air for a long while now. We had moved a step closer to achieving our dream of becoming world recognised scientists and I had Benji to thank for that!

Bessie, the Superstar doll

# Chapter Five

## The Great Discovery

I always wondered what you could achieve with peace and quiet away from Parents and the terror of the so called closely knit unit commonly known as family. The challenge we'd face was whether we'd be able to detach ourselves from the comforts of home and the embrace of the ones we truly and warmly love, latch onto the ruggedness of an old mucky shack that Benji and I would attempt to set up as our 'real' home and whether it would work out well for us. You're damn right it worked out well for us, it took us barely seconds to get over the 'initial shock'.

I never thought I nor Benji had a talent in home improvement up until now, and like they say, you'll never know until you try. So with a lick of paint here and a lick of paint there, before we knew it, we were looking at a master piece, well almost anyway. How did we achieve this? Let's just say Dad's tins of paint Alice kept batting on about DID come into good use after all along with our piggy bank savings. We had to rely heavily on our ability to improvise hence two empty wooden crates for chairs found discarded by a tip, a table with two uneven legs, same location!

We were living the absolute dream and what now lay in front of us was a testimony to that. We refocused our efforts, reinvested our sweat, blood and everything else that we could sacrifice and soon enough our proudest moment yet had finally arrived for sure. Evidence of this was in a jar in front of our eyes, and this time for the right reasons. The jar contained our very own invention made from concoction created of various bits and bobs. It was a concoction of which we were surely destined for greatness, to be the newest kids on the block as well as the richest. A formula that only two people in the whole wide world knew about so there you had it, mission accomplished.

Now due to growing fear that someone might steal our invention and cash in on our hard work, we decided that it was in our best interest not to write things down as we went along but rather leave everything stored in our magnificent brains. We know that some clever clogs have invented machines that could drain out the human brain but we would make it hard for any individual to even attempt it drain ours. I slumped into my crate chair shattered, totally exhausted but convinced all the effort invested had been worthwhile…

The stage was set, all the guests seated (including my Mum and Dad, unfortunately Alice didn't make it) even the Town's Mayor had taken his place wearing his full regalia! Surely he'd be uncomfortable sitting in this particular chair. I mean to me, he was either too big for it or it was too small for him! But you'd never have guessed the discomfort the way he beamed with a broad smile across his chubby face. You'd do well to tell him otherwise to vacate his golden Mayor's chair especially with the eyes of the world focussed on him through the lens of the camera crew from the local television station even if it was for a brief moment. I could have sworn he was eyeing up the sumptuous buffet. It was well documented that the Mayor loved a buffet or two but today it was all about someone else for a change. As if they were reading my thoughts like a book, the men were soon wise enough to up focus their attention on more picturesque viewing like for instance, the actual finalists of the scientist of the year competition i.e. us!

You would have been excused if you thought a parade was going on in the township as everywhere was bubbling with excitement. After several hundred entries the number was eventually whittled right down and what now lay on the specially created table fit for purpose contained three envelopes with the names of the finalists one of which I recognized all too well. The sides of the table were embellished with giant face shots of the greatest scientists that ever walked the earth. My idol Albert Einstein took his place alongside the likes of Alexander Bell and Louis Pasteur. From afar I had gazed proudly at the conical flask broadly marked with the number 17 for that contained our entry, weeks and weeks of mine and Benji's tears, sweat and blood. Both of us had already been ushered up to take our place amongst the other two finalists. As I watched Mrs Coburn mount the stage I knew the moment of truth was finally here. She was holding a golden envelope in her right hand.

…Ladies and Gentlemen, young scientists the moment you have been working for, waiting for is finally upon us. Contained in this envelope I have right here is the name of one of these four young scientists here (there were indeed four of us, Benji and I were the only partnership to have made it to the final). Drum roll please if you will…and the winner is …is …Daniel and Benjamin. What names did she just call, Benjamin and Daniel? Well it looks like she did. She has just come to congratulate the two of us and I can see Dad going completely berserk which was very unusual of him. Mum, she's in a flood of tears – tears of joy I presume, but back to Benji and I. I don't know about him but my feet have just turned into jelly I can barely move. Our School head has just leapt out of his seat, grabbed me and shook the life right out of me. Our school cheer leader team were actually dancing now which was a surprise as I didn't think they could. They were letting themselves go big time. Somersaulting, dancing on their heads. But they saved the very best for last as I felt someone nudge me from behind 'well done mate' a voice I was all too familiar with! Max Dillon the lead singer of The Slimes, it had to be. When I turned around I realised that I was right. How was I ever going to live this day up, Max Dillon actually touching me, wishing me all the best, Forget school, I'll be the envy of every girl in town and my shoulder will surely now be the most sacred part of me. I felt faint, ready to melt away. This was by far my best day ever!

Celebrations galore no doubt, Mrs Coburn continued in the mist of the mayhem.

'But as its customary of our winners,' she said dragging an object across the stage till she stopped by Benji and I, she appeared to lift what seemed like a rusty old bucket high above our heads then pour the contents all over us till we, our trophies and certificates were completely drenched in water. I wasn't best pleased!

'No!' I shrieked. 'Noooooooooo!'

'Dan, are you okay, Dan?'

'Hun.'

I looked around me and I'm not surrounded by a crowd of people any more. I'm actually sprawled on the floor with just Benji and the mucky hut and he's hovering over me with an empty bucket in his hand. I'm wondering what he's doing considering the fact that I'm now totally drenched.

'One minute you were talking to yourself, the next you were like a waxwork dummy on display at Madam Tussauds. Then you slumped to the ground shouting *NO*. You got me worried so I poured water over you.'

'Yes, I can clearly see that.'

Well there you have it; I'm the only person on the face of the earth who can't even daydream without suffering consequences! The up side of Benji's shenanigans was that he seemed to jolt me into action because at that point I realised a flaw with our super human brains.

However, the deed as far as we knew was done. All that was left for us to do was test our experiment and prepare to dazzle the whole school during science week and then the entire world. As Ben began to pour the contents of formula BD, the combination of both our initials, I started to daydream again (hopefully in peace this time) of what and how I would spend our first million pounds. I could see myself enter the world's famous candy store filling my pockets to the brim with the finest Slime chocolate bars that melted in your mouth like butter. The whole daydreaming image thing before me disintegrated as fast as the table in front of us as Ben poured the contents into a conical flask and some spilled over.

'Wow, this is deadly!'

Safety first was a motto that even we kids took very seriously. So here we were clagged in full regalia like true life scientists. Alright, the white overalls were a little oversized (adults size actually) but we managed to have our very own goggles and gloves that we proudly wore. All the beakers and other laboratory equipment were ours; Benji's last year's birthday present – a junior scientist kit which eventually came in handy.

'Now that's what I'm talking about. It's like real volcano larva; I think we've done it, Dan.'

I could see it now, the first people to ever create authentic homemade volcano larva, it will be sold to every shop in town throughout the country and beyond. The whole world will hear about us and our invention. We will be richer than we could ever imagine. Richer than the Queen more famous than the world's greatest football club, more globally known than The Slimes themselves!

While I was gabbing on about fame and fortune, and what it would ultimately mean for the two of us, the lava bubbled out of control, oozing out of the flask causing mayhem for a moment or two which was more than enough for us thinking safely first. We dived for cover away from the dripping lava, it was then it dawned on me that we had done a very stupid thing. Think back to the reference I made about our magnificent brains, which we relied heavily on, they weren't all that magnificent after all! They failed to highlight something of vital importance; we had only made one sample of our experiment that had now been used up demonstrating its success, we would have to make another sample mirroring the first that we would present for science week, only we hadn't written down any of the components that we had used to create the invention in the first place, yes you've rightly guessed, we were first class plonkers, soon to be stinking rich plonkers, but plonkers all the same!

The bad news didn't just end there though! Besides ruining the only table that we had in our lab; we hit the ground so hard that we damaged the already rotting wooden floor boards. In the mayhem, my foot made a gaping hole in it and to make matters worse...

'...I'm stuck! My foot is stuck in the hole,' I declared.

Despite my attempts to free my foot it wasn't budging.

'Don't panic we'll find a way, just stay calm,' Benji remarked calmly as he trudged off only to return carrying a very old looking axe over his shoulder.

It was devoid of any signs of life. The wooden handle was so rotten and termite ridden that it seemed to wobble in his grasp. The edges were blunt and very rusty.

'Here we are.'

'What do you think you're doing, Benji?'

'This old axe I've just found in the cupboard over there might just come in handy. One big swing of this and you'll be out in no time. What do you reckon?'

'I reckon no thanks,' I declared as I desperately wriggled harder with my leg hoping and praying that one more wriggle would just be enough. One swipe of that rusty old thing near my leg and I'll be out of time!

'It's either this or we do it the old fashioned way Dan, your choice.'

It was easy for him to say, stay calm and all that. He'd forgotten that it was my foot stuck in a hole not his! But not wanting to make a mountain out of a mole hole, his words not mine, I opted for the old fashioned way and made a suggestion of my own, one that wouldn't put me nor any part of my body at risk of harm. To my utmost relief, immediately the old rusty axe disappeared out of sight. Benji commanded that at the count of three we were both to heave at my mere foot with the hope that our combined strength would be enough to free it from this man-sucking man hole with limited damage done. Benji didn't wait for the three count and just hacked at my leg on two completely releasing my foot. I argued with him on why we agreed on a three count and he went on two and how I could have lost my leg. He wanted me to look on the bright side, show him gratitude and just be happy that my leg was freed all in one piece. All the above was something I found very hard to do but in the mist of our argument, we discovered something very interesting!

'Hang on what's this?' he declared.

I took my goggles off to enable me a better view. As I got up and dusted myself down, I needed a story to come up with for my parents as to why I left home with a neatly ironed pair of trousers to return as if I had been working on a building site!'

'It looks like a false panel, and it's moveable. There's something in it. I can't quite get it yet but I can feel it.'

'Stretch a bit more then.'

'I will do if you just stop barking instructions at me for once.'

'Suit yourself.'

'Got it, I'll just tug at it and with a bit of luck, it should come out.'

'Just be careful, we don't want your hand stuck in it and all but I wouldn't worry, we still have that axe!'

'Very funny, there you go.'

Now Benji was being the sarcastic one!

'What is it?'

'It's a piece of paper, all folded up.'

I said this as I blew away the dust that had settled on it.

'Unravel it and let's see what it is.'

Due to our excitement to find out what the piece of paper contained, we almost tore it into two having both grabbed it at the same time and from its timid edges.

'It looks like some sort of map.'

'It is a map, a treasure map.'

'A treasure map! Are you sure about that?'

'I think I know a treasure map when I see one.'

'Let's have a better look.'

Benji lost his goggles at this point too.

'I do know what a map looks like. I mean, it's got a well-designed plan of a certain area clearly marked with an X. Look there. All we have to do is work out the map, its location, find the treasure now how hard can that be?'

'Wow! You're right, but who would hide a map underneath wooden panels in a rotting shed?'

'You did say the shed was very old, probably been here a very long time, do the maths.'

'Do you think it's a...wow, a real treasure map? I suppose they'll be real treasure where that X is marked.'

'That is the whole idea of a treasure map.'

'So I guess we tell our parents then?'

'Don't be stupid, like they'll believe us. You know what parents are like. Remind yourself again how we came up with this place?'

'How about our school mates, they're sure to believe us.'

I stared at Ben and the look gave the message away.

'I guess we're not telling the police either huh?'
I shook my head.

'So what do we do then?'

'Well like my dad always says, if you have nothing to say, don't say it. If you want to be a real man, act like one and what do real men do?

'Find the treasure.'

'Now you're thinking like a real man. We find the treasure ourselves exactly. Forget scientists of the year; forget being the richest kids in the community, about being local heroes.'

I was now thinking big and I mean big.

'We pull this off and find the pot of gold; we'll be National heroes, we might even get to visit the Queen!'

'The Queen!'

Benji liked the sound of that and so did I.

'Now you're talking, think big!'

What a thought that would be. Ben's eyes lit up over the potential rewards that lay awaiting us. The way he stood stiff as a waxwork dummy, it was as if he was already staring at a pot of gold.

'But how are you so sure that it's a pot of gold?'

'Behind an X, there is always a pot of gold, everyone knows that.'

'Now first, we need to keep this in a safe place.'

'Yeah you're right.'

'What are you doing?'

'I'm putting it back where we found it.'

'Don't be daft, I said a safe place.'

I snatched the map off Benji, had another good look at it before I rolled it into a scroll and concealed it in my school bag.

'There, all we do now is act normal, go about our own business as usual and keep our mouths shut. What we have here is between you and me not another soul must find out and I mean that! 'Don't say anything; don't do anything until I tell you to, agreed?'

Benji agreed, well he had no choice. I was his best friend and as the title suggests, I knew best! We also agreed that this was OUR secret and no one was to find out until the day we die and even on our death beds we wouldn't reveal it to a single soul; it was simply a secret, classified information for the best friends in the world and absolutely no one whatsoever was going to be in on it except the two of us.

Ben and Dan

# Chapter Six

## Three's Company

'What are you boys whispering about?'

My bedroom door suddenly flung open, Alice barged in unannounced as usual. She was clutching her superstar doll in one hand (I have already established that she never went anywhere without it) and was holding her favourite pink comb in the other.

'Nothing,' Benji retorted.

'Yeah, mind your own business. Nothing's happening so there, now get out of my room' I demanded.

'Huh huh?'

'Huh huh what, just get out?'

'No not until you tell me what's going on?'

'We're just playing a board game.'

'Huh huh, only I can't see a board.'

Alice was yanking the hair out of her tattered dolls head with the pink comb that she had wasted a lot of her time decorating with glittery bits and bobs. She clearly had nothing better to do. Chunks of dolls hair was flying about in the most sacred and treasured part of the house and this was getting very annoying for me to bear.

'I said get out of my room Alice; take your snarly nose elsewhere and your block headed rag doll with you' I remarked as I tried to snatch it off her. She manoeuvred stylishly – she was really getting used to this, and no matter how hard I tried, she was one step ahead of me.

'Mum, Dad, Dan called Bessie a block head,' she screamed. 'How many times do I need to tell you she is not just a doll, she's a superstar doll, you munchkin,' Alice turned to me and bellowed.

'I don't care, just get out.'

'No,' she replied calmly.

'Mum, Alice is winding me up again. She won't get out of my bedroom; she's disturbing me calling me munchkin head,' I bellowed back.

I hoped that either Mum or Dad would get off their mobile phones they seemed to be on forever and a day, dash upstairs and chuck Alice out of my space, like that was going to happen! While I was hoping in vain, questions started to occupy my mind, how could she be my sister? I for one would never have guessed, we were so totally unalike, our tastes were completely different. She was a fan of the Red Petals, I the Slimes, she likes the colour purple and I love black. I like WWWF wrestling and she hates sports.

'Nah, we can't be!'

The other day I finally dared to warn Mum and Dad of a nightmare I recently had of how Alice was abducted by a family of Aliens, and how possible it is that the way she acts, which is likened to Aliens, clearly suggests that she is one and that my dream was actually real. I also came up with an alternative theory that she was adopted from a pack of wild hyenas hence her annoying laugh hence there was no possible way we could ever be related.

Due to my findings, I was grounded for a week. And as a result of my gleeful willingness to share such findings with everyone despite how upsetting it might be for 'fragile' Alice, a couple more days was added for good measure. So forgive me if the sight of my 'dearest' sister was the last thing I needed right now. Having said that, maybe I didn't even need Mum's or Dad's presence, knowing my luck, they would only come upstairs and rather than tell Alice off and give me the praise, I'd get the telling off and her the praise! So when it was evident that help wasn't forthcoming, I decided to take matters into my own hands in the most simplest of manners by pointing to the door that Alice had thoughtlessly left wide open.

'Alice, get out of my bedroom right now or else…'

'You're both up to something.'

'It's big boys' stuff, you won't understand,' Ben bleated.

'Big boys' stuff, I won't understand huh?' Alice smirked.

'Well I'm sure Dad will. Dad, there's something you need to know.'

She screamed at the top of her voice making a tune out of it as she normally does when she tells tales. With that Alice stormed out of my bedroom in a shot, I immediately pursued her. She was quick as lightening leaving my room and slamming the door at the same time that she almost took my head off. I returned with my fingers holding tight to the fringe of her dress. I dragged her in as if she was a rag doll, dumped her to the ground in a heap and shut the door behind her.

'You're both still whispering. So you are up to something well that's great, Mum and Dad must hear this. Mum, Dad!'

Well didn't I warn you that Alice was a pest? Benji and I frantically muffled her shouts with the palms of our now sweaty hands and motioned for her to be quiet. She didn't hide the fact that she was disgusted at the act of having our dirty hands anywhere near her mouth by the way she was gagging but it was a risk we had to take. Unknown to her more was guaranteed to come her way if she failed to cooperate.

'Well, what is it you guys have to say for yourselves?'

She looked annoyed! Spare a thought for me as I just had to endure the abominable sight of Alice suddenly snatching my precious Slime duvet cover off my bed to clean her nasty mouth as if she had been poisoned. To add insult to injury, she then flung it to the floor discarding it like it was trash. Of all things in my bedroom that she could have used, it just had to be the very item on view that I cherished the most! All the while Benji motioned at me to say something but first I needed to compose myself over the initial shock of what Alice had just done to my ego and that was no mean feat. And by the way, if Alice was actually waiting for an apology then she'd be waiting a lifetime especially after what she'd just done. No sooner had I found it in my heart to forgive my sister's naivety was I then in the mood to talk.

'Maybe you better tell her. It's best coming from you; after all, she is your sister.'

Are you mad I thought to myself? Did I really have to lecture Benji on why it was a very bad idea, no, catastrophic idea to let Alice in on this?

'Well, are you telling me or not? 'Alice stood arms folded as if we were wasting her time.

Oh how I was getting sick of this.

'Okay, okay you win, Alice, since you ask me nicely but this is classified top secret. You are not to tell a living soul and I mean it.'

'Aha, I knew it,' Alice cried out springing about and smirking as if she was a jack in the box. 'The look on you boys' faces gave it away,' she continued.

I guess Alice's triumphant victory dance around my bedroom had just made Benji realise what I had been trying to tell him all along about how Alice was the biggest drama queen around. If anyone had the ability to be solemn one moment then joyous the next in a heartbeat so fast that if you blinked you'd miss it Alice did, but I guess it was too late now.

'On second thoughts, do you really think it's wise that we tell her, Dan, after all you did say your sister has a big mouth?'

'What, you said that?'

'Big mouth or no big mouth, Ben, it's too late now we have no choice. I have to trust her on this one; after all, like you said she is my sister and she deserves the right to know'.

From the corner of my eye I could see Alice pull her tongue at Benji, another one of her annoying habits, the ability to blow raspberries at a time inconvenient for others but always most definitely convenient for her!

'What happened to the pact we had about how this information was only to be shared between us two and us two only!'

I knew better than Benji how ugly it was to be in this position, trust me I knew. She was my sister and I had been surrounded by situations as these all my life but I was actually trying out what is known as reverse psychology on Alice with the hope that for the first time in her life and what might possibly be the last, I'd get her on side. That she would keep her mouth shut and not gab to anyone about our latest discovery. A big risk but one I had to take and anyway let's not forget that he gave the whole secret away in the first place. The moment Alice barged in Benji had this stupid smirk of guilt written all over his face, she could read him like a book. So if things do eventually go wrong and backfire on us, I'd quickly remind him that guilt should be knocking on his door rather than mine!

'What we are about to tell you Alice does not get out of my bedroom and I mean it, because if it does…'

I opened my bedroom door, popped my head out, and checked that no one was around except us three. I closed the door again.

'…I mean it Alice, one word out of you to Mum or Dad then everyone in school will know you fancy Roger.'

'Roger! Who said I fancied Roger. I never told you that I… Have you been snooping around in my room?'

'No! Why would I do that? Now shut up and listen.'

'You have, you've been reading my diary…'

'A-l-i-c-e!'

I screamed at the top of my voice hoping for once to get Alice's full attention which eventually I was able to do.

'Just sit down, shut up and listen.'

Once Alice finally sat down and I felt she was ready to take it all in, I composed myself then let her in on our little secret…

'Ben and I, we have found a map.'

'A map! That's it?'

'Well that's NOT just it though.'

I mimicked Alice's very annoying sarcastic voice and though I hadn't yet said much, I was already beginning to regret my decision to tell her.

'Yeah well it's not just any ordinary map.'

'What kind of map is it then, a treasure map?'

Both Benji and I exchanged glances at each other in wonder as if to suggest that my sister might be an alien after all.

'Yes in fact, it is a treasure map.'

'Treasure map?'

Alice hesitated for a while, her face lit up in excitement.

'You mean a treasure map, as in a real treasure map?'

That definitely caught Alice's attention as I knew it would.

'Yes.'

'As in treasure island treasure map?'

'Yes.'

Every time I was forced to repeat myself I tried not to lose my cool-as-you-like nerve with Alice, a challenge I battled with on a daily basis. If anyone had the ability to make me dare lose my rag against my wish, it was her. Alice hesitated again her face could not have been more serious looking. Suddenly like a bolt out of the blue she roared into the most ridiculously annoying laugh I have heard in a long while. She surprised Benji, she didn't surprise me! I had heard her laugh several times over but this one; it topped the lot. She then stopped like a robot that had run out of power.

'Sorry, guys, I just had to do that. I'm not going to laugh again promise.'

Then guess what she did next? Correct, she laughed again, louder, more annoying. She laughed so hard till she went red in the face. That was it, now I regretted telling her and that was official!

'Where did you find this map, on a shipwrecked boat in the local stream?' she continued.

The local stream that ran through the township was so shallow; you could actually see what colour the pebbles at the bottom of it were. Who on earth was I kidding, Alice she was never going to change! So while she was filling her boots with laughter and making a mockery of me, I just felt so relieved and glad that I heeded Benji's advice not to share our discovery with the kids at School, and for this particular reason.

'I told you we should never have told her.'

'You were right, get out my room, Alice, NOW and remember what I said, you didn't hear a thing.'

'About what?'

'Exactly.'

'Don't worry, your secret's safe with me, treasure map, ha!'

'ALICE!'

'I'm kidding but are you sure it's not one of those you know, Dora maps that leads to a bag of you know, chocolate coins.'

She continued her annoying laughter. 'Alice, you think you're funny when you're not. Just get out of my room now.'

'She'll tell your Dad.'

'I'll take the risk now GET OUT!'

Ben couldn't so he dragged Alice who had stupidly been standing at my door entrance yapping away even though I told her several times to either come in or stay out. He shut the door behind her, whipped the map from within my bag and spread it open in front of her.

'There, see it for yourself. Does this look like a Dora map to you?'

Amazingly, that did the trick. Alice had her eyes transfixed on the map as if it was the latest superstar doll and she had also stopped laughing too… result!

'Wow, it's real treasure.'

'Of course, just like we told you,' I said decisively as I snatched the map from Alice's glare.

'What do we do now?'

'If we means you, then absolutely nothing, you do nothing besides keep your mouth shut. Us two, that's Benji and I, we are going to decipher this map, find the hidden treasure and be rich for life.'

'Can I help?'

'Yeah, like I said just act normal and keep your mouth shut. C'mon Benji, let's go.'

'No I mean can I help to find the treasure.'

'No, Alice, NO WAY.'

'Pleaseeeeeeeeeeeee.'

'No.'

'I promise to behave.'

'And I said no.'

'Come on, Dan, stop being tight.'

'I'm not being tight. No is my final word. She'll sell us out. Every time Alice decides to get involved in my business something goes wrong and you know that. It's like the hair on her doll's head. Just look at the state of it. Her hair used to be its pride and joy but look at it now, it's as bald as ET yet she can't even see it!'

'Shut up, meanie, Bessie does not appreciate you talking about her like that.'

'Go on, Dan, Let's take her.'

'No, it's not worth it, Alice all she does all day is call me names and be in my face all day and... every day.'

'Well then I will have to spill the beans to Mum and Dad, you faceless blob.'

'Told you, what did I say? Alice you wouldn't dare, you said you wouldn't tell, you just pledged an oath.'

'Please let me help I promise to be good and I'll stay out of your way and out of trouble.'

'It's bad enough that I've told you about the map in the first place, a map by the way that you dismissed and said we were day dreaming.'

'But you're just being mean. All I want to do is help.'

'The more you stay out of this the better for us all, and you know that.'

'Oh please let me come.'

Did my sister seriously not know the meaning of the word no as in definitely not, will not, shall not, cannot, something I had been repeating over and over again so many times I was sounding like a broken record? I had been speaking in clear English so what part did she not understand?!

'Alice, you know that every time you offer to help, something goes terribly wrong and I end up counting my losses. Well, I can't take that risk, not this time anyway.'

'If you're talking about who fed the fish biscuits Dan, that was you not me.'

'I'm not talking about that.'

'And it was also you who hid fish in Dad's car for an Aprils fool joke.'

'Not talking about that either.'

'C'mon, Dan, what harm can your sister do now that she knows about the map?'

Check him out, such rich words from the mouth of someone who doesn't even know my sister the way I do. Well despite their wayward pleas, I told them both for the millionth time that it was a big fat No and that was my final answer. Alice was a liability for these kinds of occasions and I was not going to budge no matter what they said, little sister of mine or not! I made it clear that when I put my foot down, I put my foot down which meant when I said NO that was exactly what I MEANT just that, NO!

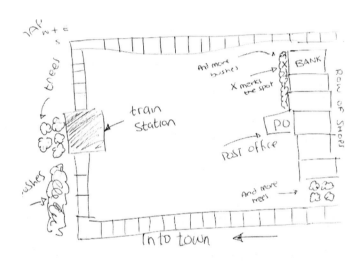

N
W + E
S

trees

train
station

And more
bushes

X

BANK

X marks
the spot

ROW OF SHOPS

PO

POST office

And more
trees

bushes

Into town ←

# Chapter Seven

## Giant Oak Tree

We had studied hard the map and all the symbols on it, finding them in real life were proving harder than we thought. Hours that should have been invested in completing our school project was spent looking around for clues that would help us decode the map. We had concluded that the best hope we would have in finding the treasure was to search and find the oak tree that was clearly highlighted on the map as being situated next to the local train station. The town only had one train station so we knew our starting point and we knew the marker on the map was indicating a train. It was marked down with two thick parallel squiggly lines that crossed over each other. That most definitely had to be the train tracks.

Locating an oak tree should have been a piece of cake, but locating such a tree in the middle of the hustle and bustle of the town centre, that was our greatest challenge, something even we did not anticipate…

'This is getting silly now.'

'Just keep searching.'

'I'm thirsty, I need a drink.'

'Are you up for this or not?'

'Are you sure that you read the map correctly?'

Never answer a question with a question Alice!

'Alice, can we just keep on searching for the big oak tree…you promised to keep your mouth shut if I let you in on this adventure. Can we keep to that promise because all you've done since we got it here has been to yap, yap, yap and I'm beginning to regret my decision already? We are simply looking for an oak tree so can we just focus on that please…'

'…I'm just asking, is it an oak tree with lots of leaves on it or not. I know you've said it a million times but I just need to be sure, that's all. I mean, I am looking for it but I'm just saying…'

'…Alice!'

'Okay, stay cool, jeepers!'

'Well Benji, I told you that it would be a waste of time her coming with us, you thought otherwise, so don't even think about complaining right now cos I know you've been itching to say something.'

Just so you know it is actually Alice my sister accompanying us on our quest for the treasure. Benji had called me aside the other day when Alice was begging like a dog after a bone. He said how it would be in the best of our interest to take Alice along with us. I obviously asked him to give me three good reasons why he thought so and he came up with the following –

'One, she won't sell us out because she'll become one of us. Two, you can keep your eye on her…

SOLD! I needed no more reasons. Okay I didn't really warm to the idea of having to split the treasure three ways rather than two but I guess I could live with that!

'Yeah you know what; maybe she's right. Perhaps she has got a point.'

'What, don't you start!'

'Well, you did say according to the map we were searching for a particular tree. But look around you, there isn't a certain tree in sight but there are MANY trees that look alike, and we are in the middle of the town centre; even if we find the oak tree, remember we are looking for a giant oak tree. And even if we find it there's a small, well, maybe large case of having to dig it up in broad daylight. And don't tell me we're are going to dig it up in broad daylight'

'Well we are going to dig it up in broad daylight.'

'I told you not to tell me that.'

'I'm sorry; I'm I missing something here. If we want to find the gold then we have to dig for it.'

'But we're kids, how are we going to do this. We can't even lift up a spade.'

'Look, enough of the talk. We'll deal with it when we get to that bridge.'

By the look on both Benji and Alice's faces, they had reached that bridge already.

There was too much dilly dallying going on for my liking, too many questions and hardly any work done. I therefore arrived at the timely conclusion that if you desperately wanted something doing properly then you had to do it yourself! So with that in mind I brushed both best friend and fiend of a sister to one side, produced the map which I placed it on the bark of the nearest tree which I leaned against. I wasn't exactly discreet but with the two blockheads, did I really need to be! I gazed at the map like I was meditating. If anyone was ready for action, that would be me!

'Right let me tell you both a bit about the art of map reading.'

'Oh here we go,' Alice said indignantly.

'The fact that a map symbolises one tree does not mean we are looking for a single tree on its own. It's a marker. The tree will look different to others and you'll be able to single it out. It's an intelligent way and act of deceit so only certain people will be able to locate the treasure. People like me while others would get dissuaded, give up and go home, people like you and Alice.'

This peoples, is a map, an actual MAP and what does a map have? It has signposts such as this and this and this. Signposts lead to clues and clues lead to treasure.

Both Alice and Benji seemed far impressed with my leadership and looked to have lost track of what I had been saying about the map or anything else. They were both staring into the sky observing the birds, clouds or whatever it was they were doing. It was clear they were concentrating more on the way they had been spoken to like they were being treated as being thick. I didn't like the idea either but I wasn't complaining rather I was proving that I was NOT.

Alice had already identified how we'd been walking around in circles for days on end without any success. If I can remember quite right when describing the extent of her dizziness her exact words were 'It's like a daze with everything around us spinning except THAT tree,' so where on earth was the cutting edge we had talked about! If we wanted to be heroes then we had to act like heroes, develop thick skin like heroes, battle through come rain or shine like heroes. Okay wait, one thing I didn't want was for either of these two to lose interest but to stay focused or I could kiss this mini adventure goodbye, that wasn't really my concern, losing out on the gold was!

'Why not, I mean we have to find it first, its treasure that we are on about here, gold coins, we want to be rich don't we, or is that just me? Look, we're kids anyway, what do people do when it comes to kids, exactly they ignore us, no one has time for kids these days but if anyone does ask, we're on a nature trail, got that Alice?'

'Whatever you say, but I'm with Alice on this one. Digging up trees in the town centre, I don't like the sound of that.'

'Will you just keep on searching or.'

Dan what on earth are you doing? You don't buy loyalty in this way. Buy...of course!

'Tell you what, Alice, let's buy you that drink you wanted, milkshake king-size yeah?'

'Well yeah.'

I bet Alice was wondering why the change of heart.

'And you, Benji the kids wonder meal you asked for.'

'Oh I don't remember...'

'Yes you did c'mon. As a matter of fact, I'm feeling very generous today so we can all have a wonder meal. You've worked hard for it so let's go with it!'

The refreshment break did the trick, it burnt a hole in my pocket considering the fact they had only been on the job barely five minutes and I had already spent most of my money on our little investment but who was I to complain. Anyway, I needed a refreshing start and they came back exactly that...refreshed and ready for action!

'Hey how about that tree over there, it looks odd!'

'No, it's not what we are looking for, not according to the map see, nothing like it.'

'How are you so sure, a tree's a tree I would have thought.'

'Do you want to be rich or not.'

'Yes.'

'Well then, keep your thoughts to yourself, less talk and more work.'

Alice was pulling her tongue at me. I could tell as I had eyes at the back of my head!

'A-L-I-C-E!'

'C'mon Alice, let's keep searching…'

Benji was pulling Alice away but she was having none of it.

'I told you that they all look the same.'

'I'm not blind you know, just keep on searching…'

And so we did for what seemed like days on end, our attempts at finding this elusive tree was like searching for a needle in a haystack. Our hopes of turning from dull kids into super rich kids overnight was disintegrating faster than the money on Dad's credit card!

The following day in school I spent a chunk of my time focussing on why it was so difficult to find anything that had been drawn on the map. It had crossed my mind over and over and over again that maybe, as Alice and Benji had suggested like a trillion times (even if only a slim chance) that maybe we actually were on a wild goose chase and that it was high time we let Mum and Dad in on our secret and who knows parents' help (no matter how ancient that might be) could come in handy after all. They might even earn themselves a few quid for the honour! Something that would surely put a smile on Mum's face for her next shopping spree! I would use Mr Bonesworth's History class to continue daydreaming of how, against all odds, we eventually find the pot of gold underneath the oak tree that magically appeared in my garden one sunny day.

<u>Bio Fact</u>

Name: Mr Alexander Reginald Bonesworth
Age: 100BC!
Nickname: Unknown
Hobbies: Digging deep into the historical archives
Most interesting fact: His class is borrrringgggg!

History was my most boring class ever! Why I hear you say? For one, why it was ever created I would never know. I mean, of what interest was the country's past and as a matter of fact, anybody else's? Silly me, here I am thinking it's all about the future, the here and now (Says a lot about what I know!) It was pointless, useless, needless, meaningless and a total bore with a capital B.

I found it so boring I reckoned if I was smart enough, the hours Mum and Dad would deprive me of everyday to wake up early to prepare for school I could get back in this class. Being the smart person that I am, I did! It would start with a cheeky snooze with my eyes just about wide enough to convince the History teacher that I wasn't sleeping even though I was. I would then graduate to the tilting of the head to shoulder as if I was seeking help from a class mate. When it was evident that I was getting away with it, I went for the book standing on desk trick, where I looked to be highly interested in the class discussion, even appearing to read the book when clearly I wasn't. I knew the tricks of the trade, if any did, it was I. Wherever there was a will, there was a way and I would find that other way, I didn't disappoint!

On this occasion, history class was overwhelming boring, so much so, it barely took long before I had lift off. Soon enough, Mr Bonesworth and the rest of the class, were nothing to me but a daze. I could just about hear the Teacher's voice which was by now all muffled and sounded like it was coming from a transistor radio that had been dumped at the bottom of a river.

'Now, class, today we are doing something different. Let's talk historical facts about our dear community. I'm sure several questions will be popping into your heads as I speak.'

Definitely not my head!

'Questions about what our community used to be like many years ago and the relevance it has in today's society,'

*Well, I can answer that here and now. None, none, and none.*

'You'll be glad to know that I aim to answer those questions and more over the next few weeks. Any questions class?'

You could hear a pin drop.

'Okay today it's all about our community and transportation, what was, used to be and is now. So without further ado, take out your History, Me and My Community books, the one written by P.C Bore...'

*Exactly*

'...and turn to page 14.'

OH OOH, I had a slight problem. I couldn't turn to page 14, in fact, I couldn't turn to any page at all simply because I didn't have the book, well not anymore anyway.

Remember my botched experiment of the other day, well I needed a hard platform to place it on and store away. This particular book fitted the bill, it had a hard back, it was big enough, it was strong enough so I sacrificed it, however it was not spill-prove enough. When the contents of my master class experiment was ruined by the combined efforts of Benji, Alice AND Mum, this particular book took the hit!

Once the well-documented disaster occurred I could hardly touch it let alone open it! It was gooey from back to front, up, down whichever way you looked at it. Telling Mum and Dad about it would have meant another lecture which I was keen to avoid at all costs. So I did the best thing I could with it. Let's just say right this moment it's being buried in one of the country's landfills. Now how ironic is such fate for a history book!


But knowing me, I never ever let a dull moment bring me down. Mr Bonesworth was short-sighted hence the glasses he wore that made him look like a 1960's geek. I put two and two together and logically was confident that there would be no way on earth he would notice my Football World annual even with all its bright colours!

'…So as a former mining town those many years ago the main stay commodity for the people was coal. As you well know, coal was the main source of power for the trains and also source of energy for the Nation at the time. People relied heavily on coal for cooking and heating during the winter. Now the coal would be dug up from the mines and the shafts used to transport the coal to places where it was easily assessable to be sold. These shafts obviously were known as coal shafts…' blah! blah! blah!

Mr Bonesworth asked if there were any questions. Around about this time I and half the class would have switched off.

'Sir, I have a question.'

Everyone that is except Roger whom the class nicknamed CCR. It sounded like some sort of incurable disease I know, but it actually stood for Clever Clogs Roger. A title he was well worthy of due to fact he always had a question to ask for everything regardless of the subject matter. If your teacher challenges you to ask a question no matter how silly it sounds this is what you get if you have a knack for coming up with some answer all of the time!

'Sir, are there coal shafts in this town,' he bleated from out of the blue.

'Very good Roger, never unusual for you to have an interest in anything historical, so yes I believe that there used to be a shaft running under the town for a few miles, as a matter of fact, it's still there I'm made to believe, no longer in use but a good example of the importance of coal as a source of energy and means of transportation, well done. So class as I was saying…'

That's about all that I got from the coal and shaft debate. I was smart enough as it was and I didn't need history classes to remind me. The only problem with being smart is that you actually need to have eyes at the back of your head which clearly I didn't or I probably would have noticed Benji waving furiously at me trying hard to get my attention while I was determined to doze off yet again with the hope I'd do so uninterrupted. I guess he wanted to inform me of the teacher's presence looming around me. I waved nonchalantly back at him. He was trying to relay a message to me and I had one for him n'all, which was to leave me alone and let me enjoy my nap. Well, I succeeded in neither. Mr Bonesworth continued his investigation into the noticeable intermittent snoring that was clear to him and the rest of the class and it was obvious where it was coming from! Arms on table, head in arms, I was in dreamland but when I woke up I was soon in horror land! There I was stood like a condemned convict in front of the school Principal who was demanding to know why I was catching 40 winks and decided to do that in the history class. I thought it was blatantly obvious but again what do I know! I had no immediate answer for him but he had one for me in the form of a letter to my parents (the second one in recent time). This would be solid confirmation for me, if ever I needed one, that my forth coming birthday party was, mildly putting it, h-i-s-t-o-r-y.

I didn't let the latest development in my short life dampen my mood or anyone else's so I met up with both Alice and Benji during School lunchtime as planned. I wouldn't be one to bother them with news flash about me, knowing the School for what it was worth, they would have somehow found out already, and they had! But all three of us had bigger fish to fry…

'It can't be the railway track can it?'

'Alice, we are not going through that again, we've been there before too many times for my liking.'

'Hang on, Dan; I thought you wanted to share something with us?'

'Yeah.'

'Well don't keep us waiting will you, spit it out.'

'Is it about the map?'

'Will you keep your voices down someone might hear us.'

'It is about the map?'

'Is it or isn't it?'

'Obviously.'

'Well then.'

'Have you found the treasure without us?'

'He has you know, it's that silly smirk on his face, can't you tell.'

'I knew you couldn't be trusted you traitor.'

Both Alice and Benji looked at me in utter disgust. I was like a bag of rubbish they just wanted to get rid.

'Keep your voices down, shut up and listen. No I haven't found the treasure but I have found the oak tree.'

'What?'

'How?'

'We were actually barking up the wrong tree.'

'What are you talking about?'

'The map, you know those thick lines that run across it, from one side of town to the other?'

'Yeah.'

'We had no luck locating the oak tree by the train tracks remember.'

'Yes and also remember it was you that said it was our starting point.'

'I miscalculated, it's easily done but listen to this right, you know I talked about markers used on maps to aid explorers, yeah?''

'Well we're not surprised you got it horribly wrong now are we?' Alice said as she pointed to both her and Benji.

*No surprises there.*

'What.'

'Oh what a waste of space you are, Ben. You just had to locate the wrong tree and waste everyone's time. It's so typical of you to do this. I know how to read a map, he said. I know what markers are, where and how we can find them. With someone like you in charge, who needs a map, with your brains we'll be alright So what are you going to tell us now, let me guess, we've got the wrong map!'

'Will you stop your moaning and whining for a second both of you, especially you Alice. Hear me out and I DO know what I'm talking about!'

They didn't look convinced but I continued all the same.

'The symbol of the church is directly adjacent to the symbol of the oak tree. When you stand at the church entrance there is only one tree that is in view point and it's an oak tree so that's got to be our marker and starting point. If you're not with me on this one, you never will.'

They both shook their heads slowly. AND NO they definitely weren't with me.

I looked around and as no one else was present except three of us I produced the map and circled in what I had been trying to say.

This was my only hope.

'There you go, have a look at this for yourselves. The position of the oak tree from the local church and the next symbol on the map clearly forms the famous eagle's eye. This is proof, that our starting point is right here.

I prodded the map so heavily with my pencil I almost put a hole straight through it.

'So this is what all the excitement's about?'

'Is it not worth the excitement?'

Looking at the dull faces of the miserable two, probably not.

'I'm going back to my class before I get into trouble.'

'Me too.'

'Thanks for you vote of confidence guys, you're very welcome. It's nice to know you have very little faith in me.'

'Our faith in you didn't go very far, blame yourself for that.'

'You can talk, Alice; you weren't supposed to be on this adventure anyway.'

'Your sister's right, Ben, you can be big headed at times you know. C'mon Alice, let's go.'

They both left but not until Alice pulled her tongue at me before skipping away. It was then that it suddenly occurred to me that Alice and Benji, sister and best friend they might be, they were also hard work. Nevertheless, being the leader I had to be the bigger person, show them the way even if it meant being down trodden on such a day as today. I knew at the back of my mind that it would be a sacrifice worth taking in the end and I would gladly accept their apologies for not believing in me no matter how long it would take. So I decided that in the interest of us all we would forge ahead in our quest to find the hidden treasure and our starting point would most definitely be THAT oak tree whether they liked it or not!

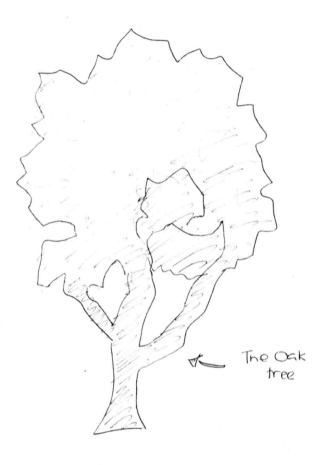

The Oak tree

# Chapter Eight

## Birthday Treat

My twelfth birthday went as quickly as it came. If I had blinked I would have missed it! I had forgotten about all my endeavours from weeks passed that I had unwittingly piled up but a few people hadn't. Dad hadn't forgotten, Mum hadn't forgotten and Alice definitely hadn't forgotten. The story of my life from a third eye, it was presented to me, gift wrapped, laid right in front of me, like a dagger through my heart, well at least that's what it felt like! The things I had and hadn't done, everything was accounted for, the things I said and never said and more, all was revealed. It was like watching the playback of my life but in reverse, like payback time, paying back but with so much added interest! The threats, I mean, I had long lived with them but for my family to stoop so low and actually put them into action! Unbelievable! I will forever take their words, from now on with a pinch of salt!

So anyway, true to my parent's words and Alice's, too, it was definitely payback and in a year of 365 days or 366 whichever way, they just happened to pick the day of my birth to ruin my entire life. What better way to payback eh!

First and foremost, the party should have been held in a venue of my choice but spectacularly it was cancelled due to unforeseen circumstances.

'You seem to be having bad luck, son.'

No arguments there considering the fact that all ten venues cancelled due to the exact same reason!

My kind hearted parents suggested having the party at home where there would be no risk of cancellations and since that was the only other option, other than to scrap the whole idea I kind of agreed.

I was intrigued as to how they'd explain a birthday party without any proper music. Mum insisted that we play the best of the 90's greatest hits. Dad threatened to take us a few decades back the opposite direction and gleefully whipped out his archaic Bay City Rollers on vinyl. He was excited at the prospect of trying out the out of sorts Juke box he got for Christmas from a jumble sale maybe! Mum, she wasn't having any of it but Dad, he wasn't willing to let go! So while they were engaged in their little squabble forgetting the real reason for the celebrations, I gave them a gentle reminder that if anyone would be selecting any form of music it would be me h-e-l-l-o, the birthday boy. With that finally cleared up I didn't hesitate to make the 'junk' box, 90's collection along with the Bay City 'slickers' record all disappear never to resurface in a long while( at least not until the end of my party anyway) to be replaced by, you guessed it, The Slimes current number one album and my favourite song 'disaster.'

We are the Slime
We're going home to you
We are the Slime
What ya gonna do
Sing it from the rooftops
Sing it on the streets
Sing it in the bathroom
Sing it when you eat
Drum it in their ear holes
Drum it to your friends
Sing it to your Parents
May it never end?
Slime! Slime! Slime!

The song was sick! My mates and I were just getting all warmed when Dad made an untimely announcement that didn't go down well at all.

'Dan, turn that racket down immediately before the neighbours call the police.'

We were hit for six. Being told not to blast Slime music was like telling Tom Daley to dive into an empty pool! Slime music without the blast, it was unheard of…

'It's the Slime's, Dad, and their music is ace.'

'Their music will soon be trash because that's where it will be ending up in a bit if you don't turn it down.'

'C'mon, Dad, don't be tight!'

As I can recall, he was tight. We weren't allowed to blast out the music in fact, I was warned to turn the music all the way down. At one point we had it so low that every time the neighbours' cat meowed, we could hear it! So that's how I endured abuse from Dad for the sake of my beloved Slimes. I took one for the team. In contrast I remember Alice's last birthday party which incidentally was NOT at home. Noise! What noise…?

'Dad isn't the music a touch too loud?' I yelled.

'Sorry?'

Exactly I thought to myself.

'I said the music, it's too loud. The fish bowl's vibrating.'

'Oh don't worry about that, the glass, it's sound proof.'

'Well what about the neighbours?'

'Sorry?'

'Neighbours, what about the neighbours?' I screamed again, at this rate my head would explode but I was more worried that another excuse was coming.

'I wouldn't worry about them, they're deaf.'

Told you, funny they weren't deaf when I had my party!

'But the police, what if they come knocking on the door?'

'They were young once, I'm sure they'll understand.'

Understand, sure I get it I was living under a cloud of threat of arrest if I made too much noise during mine though. Yes it was the classic rule for one, different for another scenario and I was caught in the thick of it.

How about the guest list? How could you come up with a plan to invite some of your class mates ahead of others? Surely you are asking for trouble. Check Dad out when I confronted him with this latest dilemma I mean with parents like mine, coming up with a plan is dead easy. You just throw caution to the winds!

'Just ten friends when I have at least thirty in my class?!'

'I mean it, Dan, no more.'

'It's ten or nothing,' Mum interjected in Dad's support.

'It IS nothing.'

'D-A-N-I-E-L!'

'How do I explain to the whole class I'm limiting the number of guests?'

'Just say – class my mum and dad have limited my invites to 10 – it's that simple.'

Dad was trying to be funny but it looked like I was the joke.

'I'll be the unpopular one though. There will be mayhem!'

'Make sure you only invite ten of your mates, Dan, or there certainly WILL be mayhem,' said Mum sternly.

'Any more than ten the expense will have to come from your weekly allowance.'

What allowance?

I was getting peanuts so it didn't matter to me anyway if I was forfeiting the lot; the money wasn't worth the paper it was written on!

'We'll NOT be sticking our heads out the windows in our own home on no one's account,' she added.

Unless of course you were Alice! If I remember Alice's birthday party correctly, she could invite her whole class, not a problem with numbers there...

'Daddy, I can invite the whole class, do you really mean that?'

'Alice, honey, princess, you can invite whoever you want. Isn't that right Susan?'

'Of course, no cost spared for our baby.'

'But you said I was to keep strictly to the budget.'

'Nonsense, okay we're going over slightly but I'm sure we can patch up, sacrifice other things.'

'H-e-l-l-o! How convenient.'

I let the words slip out of my mouth but thankfully no one was listening. I daren't imagine the consequences if they did. You would have thought I already had all the punishment they could gave but I wouldn't be surprised if they came up with something else.

So it was all about Princess Alice, gorgeous Alice, never-can-do-any-wrong-Alice.

While I had to cramp my mates into our house! Alice had no such problem...

'You can open your eyes now.'

Alice moves her hands away from her face and reveals her surprise. She shrieks in utter delight as she discovers what it is. I shriek but for a totally different reason

'Bessie's Bowling BAY.'

'I CAN'T BELIEVE THIS!' We both exclaimed for totally different reasons.

'You better believe, Alice, this is really happening.'

You bet this is happening. Having just minutes ago referred to her as a nutmeg head for calling the entire school football team a bunch of jelly babies, Alice and company brushed past me as if I wasn't even there, might as well not have been.

'That's right but it's not all. Tell her, Phil.'

'Okay, this is the exciting part of the treat,' he said as he giggled like an excited 2 year old.

For her maybe and by the way, I didn't know treats came in two phases! Dad pointed to a young man who dashed over to us from what seemed like no-where. He had boyish looks and beamed with one of those smiles that started from the corner of his face and stretched all the way to the other side. It was one of those smiles I was convinced if you smacked him hard on the head he'd still be smiling. It stuck to his face and was contagious it made you want to burst out into laughter yet here I was with hardly much to laugh about.

'Hi guys.'

He waved as if he was painting an imaginary half circle in mid-air whilst stamping his left foot as if he was hopping.

'My name is Robyn.'

Like we didn't know, the name tag pinned on his chest that was bigger than my entire head definitely gave that away.

'Everyone, say hi Robyn.'

The girls were somewhat excited to see Robyn so there they all were shouting in their girlie voices…hi Robyn.

I just wanted someone to kindly pass me a bucket to throw up in.

'I'm your host and I'm going to make today the best day of your entire lives. Where I come from…'

I thought he didn't sound English.

'…we are the ultimate dream makers and I'm going to make your dream come true and you and you…'

And what place would that be?

'...I'm the original Californian guy. C'mon in, let me show you around.'

During the so called welcome presentation and while he was talking, Robyn pressed each girls head gently like he was passing along some good luck charm. When he got to me he just stopped and it was at that point he waved everyone inside, very weird. Not that it mattered much but I later learnt he used to work in the Disney world resort in Florida hence the 'I'm going to make your dreams come true' promise, must have come by way of habit!

Inside the popular but very swanky bowling centre we were ushered into a room marked royal banquet hall and this was no understatement. The table had food presentation fit, well for royalty. Hot buffet, cold buffet, different varieties of desserts, they had it all.

'So after a couple of bowling games you make yourselves down here, take care of this lot and then, follow me. You are well in for a treat today. Did I hear a whoop whoop girls?'

While the girls and Robyn were whooping away throwing their hands all over the place, is this just me but I counted three treats and here's me thinking they only come in pairs!

'You then move out and follow that path which leads you over there next to the fountain and stop right there.'

'You mean next to I&C?'

'No actually in I&C'

I&C! Now that's injustice right there. For the record I&C was every kids dream place. It was ice cream world, the haven for the best made ice-cream and waffles in town. A place of 1001 different ice cream flavours. It was so big inside you could get lost. It was so popular rumour has it that people from far and wide travelled hundreds of miles just to taste of this sought after delicacy. So Mum and Dad had only got a table for Alice and all her friends. Could her day get any better and mine any worse?! Could you ask for anything better on such a gorgeous day with the sun shining down on them? I remember my party, even the weather didn't turn up. I had thunderstorms all day long!

Well if there was any consolation for me, it would be partaking in the birthday feast Alice would enjoy. If you couldn't beat them you join them even if it would be for a brief spell. Besides the thought of the food and images of it earlier, my mouth was still watery. I would be going against my principle of dining with the enemy but I was willing to make an exception. A man who wasn't there before now stood at the Banquet Hall entrance. Why on earth was he guarding a room full of food was beyond me, he obviously didn't have anything else better to do? Well he did, stop the likes of me from entering for a start!

I enquired why and he insisted that the party was strictly a girlie party for eleven year olds as inscribed on the sign on the wall which he pointed to. (I guess that explained why no boys were invited) He correctly pointed out that I was not a girl nor did I look eleven so, on both counts I did not qualify. But wouldn't the fact that I was the celebrant's brother (older brother for that matter) be enough for me to take my rightful place in the banquet hall, be the supportive brother that I needed to be for my fragile little sister. By virtue of the fact I spent nearly the whole day in Dad's car suggested that it wasn't!

Inside Dad's car was well boring and I desperately needed to warm my dampened spirit up. Considering the circumstance, there was really only one thing to do ...

We are the Slime
We're going home to you
We are the Slime
What ya gonna do
Sing it from the rooftops
Sing it on the streets
Sing it in the bathroom
Sing it when you eat
Drum it in their ear holes
Drum it to your friends
Sing it to your Parents
May it never end?
Slime! Slime! Slime!

'Turn that CD off.'

How wrong was I!

Back to the food and how else could they explain the menu of the day for my party?! From what was laid out before me, it looked as if we were being treated to a teddy bears picnic.

'Benji are you letting go of the crisps or what? The plate of sausage rolls that went your way never came back!'

So there we were, teenagers fighting over the right for toddlers' scraps.

Flashback to Princess Alice's party...

'…a party meal fit for a princess.'

Dad's words not mine!

'Dessert is served. There you go, birthday girl, your vanilla ice cream volcanic melt down just as you ordered and topped with crunchy bits and chocolate larva for extra flavour.'

The girls thanked the attendants then shovelled into the sides of their various favoured ice cream with their giant scoopers. Ice cream splattered all over their faces, bits of toffee stuck on noses and lips. Teeth clasping together in delight as the sweet taste is much appreciated.

Okay so this was just me visualizing what might have happened since I wasn't there but I certainly was for mine!

'Right, guys, who took a scoop from my jelly and ice cream before I take action?'

'Not me.'

'Well someone did, my jelly it's still wobbling and if no one wants to own up do not be surprised if a scoop of this hits you in the eye.'

Anyway I missed but someone else didn't and that was enough to set us all off. Hence this explained the mess I had to clean up at the end.

There were a lot more how else's, but to save myself the pain, I tried to make the most of what I got which was very little. The occasion was so boring that the most memorable event of the evening, well I had a pick from two choices! It was spending hours on end cleaning all the litter that my mates had kindly left behind or when everyone gloated at my cake not because it looked spectacular, but that a fly had nestled on it and there was a bet on how long it would last there before it would eventually get swatted! Add the fact that I was made to clean up every crumb and speck of dust. Alice conveniently decided she was too occupied with other things to even offer to. My misery was well and truly complete!

I wanted to threaten Alice with her own share of the gold when we find it, if she didn't help me, definitely on my mind, but I knew she would only blab to Mum and Dad about our secret. This was something that we had done so well to keep under wraps and for so long. I didn't want anything or ANYONE to ruin our plans now, more so that I could feel we were almost there. Alice was the supreme party pooper and would have loved to hog the spotlight but she wasn't getting any of it and I would be seeing to that personally. I got everything I had wished for except tickets to see the Slimes live in concert which meant I had nothing. It was the tickets that I really wanted more than any other thing in this entire world. I had given Mum and Dad every opportunity to get the tickets as my present, all the hints I gave them and I would have thought that it would have been such a great present to acknowledge my twelve year on earth, but they didn't take that golden chance and it was my given right to know why. So boldly I enquired from my parents the reason why. I wanted a simple answer and I got one! I was told that if I could for once not make it all about me, manage to stay out of trouble, be good and maintain it between now and Christmas, I might just get surprised. I'm sure they must have mixed me up with Alice, it's easily done. Wait till Christmas to be surprised! Well if that was what it took to be surprised, then they might as well forget it! My only consolation was that I had paid my debt and was now living free, at least till the next instalment of punishment! Even if my Mum and Dad were preparing a truce, which I doubted very much, it was too late. I'll be writing personally to Santa demanding a new set of parents!

# Chapter Nine

## The Introoders

On this particular day both Mum and Dad left the house wearing long miserable faces. It wasn't unusual for one of my parents to be miserable but when both were, it would be deemed a really bad day. Nothing I ever said to my parents stuck, they did all the talking and I the listening so this time when I spoke and all they did was just grunt, I knew it wasn't just bad it was rock bottom bad. I guess whenever the postman arrives at the door step with chunks of letters marked bills, it was never going to be a good day. It didn't help that the weather wasn't great either. The dark clouds suggested that it would likely be a horrible weather day despite the fact that we were in the heart of summer. Add that to the fact that we had been wasting our time on this stupid, old map and it looked pretty bad for me too. So we were all just looking forward to finishing from school and then heading off to our little getaway for some relaxation. If we couldn't be guaranteed and enjoy the warmth of a summer's day, we would make do with the warmth of our little hideout. Besides I had been doing some serious research and I came up with some breaking news that I could hardly wait to share with Alice and Benji. It was a discovery sure to change absolutely everything for us. I know they had heard the same line from me before and were far from impressed, I was well aware of that and needed to do the spectacular. So when we (Alice and I) arrived at our lab and I was enveloped in this weird feeling that something just wasn't right and I could also feel a certain coldness, (Alice would conclude that it was more than just my sixth sense in action that it was just my usual self being stupid again) my eagerness to 'put on a show' quickly evaporated no matter what Alice had to say to convince me otherwise, though she did try her utmost best.

From the state of our hut, it seemed someone had put on a show and forgot to clean up!

I already had enough of Alice for one day (she was like the pain in the backside that just wouldn't go away) and her constant questioning, or if you like nagging wasn't helping. I wasn't ready to rise to this no matter what. I had an experiment to complete and in the mist of this the small matter of searching and finding gold and now this! Alice was clearly an attention seeker and I wasn't prepared to pay her ANY attention whatsoever!

'What was it you wanted to tell me in school but didn't?' Alice quizzed me in her usual Alice way.

'What the…'

I stopped suddenly in my tracks as I scanned the hut with my eyeballs.

'What?' Alice enquired again.

'Look at the state of this place. Why would you put that conical flask over there by the window? The sunlight could cause all sorts of damage.'

'Yes, only I didn't put it there. Maybe it was Benji.'

'No, he's a fellow scientist and knows the basic rule about exposing those kinds of flasks to sunlight. It was a direct insult aimed at Alice and she knew that was why she was frowning intently

'Typical of you guys to blame it on the girl, well sorry to disappoint but I didn't do it.'

'Are you sure you've not been messing about in here?'

'Well it could have been you.'

'Don't be daft, I would have remembered.'

'Really, you don't even remember what we had last night for tea!'

I guess that was Alice taking revenge for my earlier swipe at her and she wasted no time did she? Nice one Alice! Well like I said, it definitely wasn't me. Why would I do that? By the time we come back from the poxy treasure hunt, half the time we're knackered anyway!' She continued her rant.

'Well if it wasn't you nor me and I'm sure it wasn't Benji then it must...'

I stopped suddenly the only thing I could hear now was my heart beating fast!

'What!'

I grabbed a crate, the only make shift weapon I could find, and began to cautiously move around the room prodding it in front of me. That just happened to be its final straw as the already rotting wooden box crumbled in my hands.

'What is it, Dan?'

'I think we have intruders.'

'Intruders? Are you sure, I mean maybe its rats.' 'No matter how big rats are Alice, they can't move chairs, tables and science equipment.'

'What could it be then?'

'Eh they could be spies from school. Remember those dodgy year 8 kids we saw the other day who kept staring at us as they were kicking about in the area; told you they weren't to be trusted. They've probably been following us, spying on our experiment, wanting to rob us of our glorious moment.'

Clearly incensed that a group of thoughtless idiots could do this, I grabbed an old newspaper rolled it up till it was shaped like a baton. I smacked it against the tired looking table which shuddered. Then I waved it in front of me as if I was losing my mind.

'Well you can come out of your hiding place right out now whoever and wherever you are. Boy have you got some explaining to do. Let me warn you no funny business because I'm well prepared.'

My clear message of defiance to our unwanted guests seemed in vain. We cautiously combed the hut but found nothing that could cause any concern to us unless we'd count the moths fluttering about.

'Well, no one's here. Probably the rats like you said.'

'I don't want to be here right now, Dan.'

Alice was scared and I knew she wasn't lying. It was very rare she'd comb her doll's hair so hard that the head would start to wobble as it was doing right now.

'Neither do I, come on.'

I would leave wondering who on earth had done this to us and why. We had barely taken our first step when the door suddenly burst open. Two men waltzed in.

'Well, well, well what have we here?'

I guess that was the answer to my first question. I dared not to think of the answer to the second!

'We were actually just leaving, c'mon Alice,' I retorted as I grabbed her by the hand and headed for the door

'Not so fast kids.'

'Yeah going somewhere…kids?'

One of the men stretched his hand out to reveal a very dirty palm. The man's googly eyes stared at us without blinking as he and his colleague formed a two man wall in front of us.

'I believe you have something precious that belongs to me, I want it and I want it now!

Alice and I shared a glance at each other, gulping as we did. It looked like the day we had written off as being so bad was about to get even worse…

Clive

Igor

# Chapter Ten

## The Truth of the Matter

The two men looked like bandits straight out of a comic book. They were like misfit twins. One was very tall, huge with a long chin, crooked nose and beady eyes. He had both hands behind his back while the other was holding something under his arm. He was the threatening one, fat and stumpy with a rough deep voice, was scruffy and stunk like rotten eggs. Yeah, they were definitely a complete miss-match. The scary thing was I hadn't a clue who these men were and they were giving very little away. One thing I did know, I had to be brave, put up a strong face if anything, for the sake of protecting my little sister Alice. She on the other hand, had different ideas and maybe if I had known earlier I probably wouldn't have even bothered!

'This place, this hut, does it belong to you then?'

It was nice of Alice to start the conversation with some nonsensical stuff but I really would have preferred her to have kept her mouth shut! It was a distraction, uncalled for but I used it to full advantage nudging forward towards the direction of the front door gradually as I spoke.

'Not exactly.'

'Yeah, this isn't even yours; his mate said it's been here for years.'

I nudged forward a few steps more encouraging Alice to do the same.

'You're right.'

'I said not so fast young lady, gentleman' the short man retorted. He motioned us both to move back, we had no choice unless we were planning to barge straight through them both.

'They look like two kids to me.'

'I know what they are, you idiot. Now, a little birdie tells me that you lot have been meddling in my property.'

'At least now we know whose been meddling in ours,' I spoke boldly.

'You sure have the gift of the gab don't you?'

No, that person was Alice I was merely a pretender.

'Are you here for something?' Alice spoke trembling.

'You're right again, smart kids these two innit?'

'So if you don't own the hut, who are you?'

I spoke boldly again but didn't have a clue where that came from as within me I was shaking like a leaf from one of the several oak trees we had seen.

'Who we are is irrelevant; the question is who are you?'

The man pointed his crooked finger into our direction. Alice responded on behalf of both of us by blowing a very annoying raspberry. Yes, my sister Alice swings in roundabouts especially in the mist of adversity. Don't ask me why, she just does. I didn't have a clue where that came from and neither did the two men, they were not impressed and frankly, neither was I!

'OK, so you want to play games, let's play then.'

'Let it go.'

'They're fooling with us though.'

'They're kids. That's what kids do. I used to do that when I was a kid. And anyway, you should know.'

The tall man was left scratching his head.

'You don't want to tell me who you are, that's fine by me.'

'We don't talk to strangers.'

That's Alice again though you must have already guessed.

Fair enough. I'm missing something very valuable here, you kids wouldn't happen to know where it is would you?' the short man continued.

'Where what is?'

'No we don't.'

'He's talking about a …'

'Shut up, let me handle this. Now I left a very important insignificant scrawny piece of paper with a few diagrams here and there on it.'

'Where exactly did you leave it?'

The short man laughed then smiled sheepishly. He seemed happy to play along. . To think he was yet to lose his patience especially with Alice around, for that I had to give him a lot of credit. He pointed to the gaping hole in the floorboard, the exact spot my foot got stuck.

'Now have you seen it?'

'No.' we both answered at the same time.

'It was a piece of paper with a giant cross on it amongst other meaningless signs and symbols,' the tall man added.

'We're not silly; we DO know what a map is,' Alice bellowed.

I only prayed that she'd keep her mouth shut and let them do the talking whoever they were. Like that was ever going to happen!

'So I guess you've seen it, where is it then?'

Alice was about to continue blabbing and risk dropping us right in it, but I beat her to it. I wanted to know who these men were, that was the first rule of engagement, that when you meet someone for the very first time, you need to know who they are, and everyone knew that except my sister Alice!

'Have you heard him, the boy wants to know who we are.'

The two men roared into laughter. They somehow reminded me of Alice.

'Shall I tell him who we are, Clive?'

The stumpy man stopped laughing. When the tall man eventually noticed he was the only one in the room that had carried on giggling, he too stopped.


<u>Bio Fact</u>

Name: Clive

Age: unknown

Nickname: The Stumpy one

Hobbies: unknown

Most interesting fact: He thinks he's scary

'Idiot, I told you to always use an alias especially when we're at work.'

'What's an alias?'

'Does it really matter now, you nit wit?'

'Nit wit, I know what that is. It's someone who…'

'Oh shut up.'

Now all I needed to know was the other man's name.

'You haven't answered my question, kids.'

'You're wasting your time,' Alice replied boldly.

'Is that right?'

'Yeah that's right. My brother, Dan, is as tough as nails, you don't want to mess with him, he'll sort you out.

Well that was just g-r-e-a-t! Trust Alice to throw that one on me. She pointed right at my chest which I had since puffed out like I was superman about to launch into the sky, but despite that, my whole body was wobbling like I was made of jelly.

'Will he now, super boy ready to save the world?'

One of the men edged forward. Now hang on a second I thought to myself. Here was a situation where my sister needed me to be strong, to protect her, and be her hero. Was I up for it? Of course I was up for it… just not today! I responded to the man's movement and in turn edged backwards. The man was stopped from going any closer to me by the outstretched hand of his colleague.

'Leave him, idiot, fancy squaring up to innocent harmless kids.'

'I want Mum,' Alice thoughtfully requested.

'I want my map. Isn't life a bugger, here we are with neither!'

'Well maybe it would help if you didn't ask us the same question like a million times. You sound like a broken record and I can't think straight.'

Did it not occur to Alice that if she didn't stop talking, the only thing that would be broken around here would be us, because that was definitely obvious to me nevertheless, Alice continued her endless and fruitless gripe.

'No we haven't seen it and even if we have, you're not getting it,' she continued.

At that point I wished Alice would speak for herself and not just sometimes, all of the time, like that was ever going to happen! Clive grinned and showed his horrible set of green stained teeth.

'I said where is the map and I would suggest you start talking before my patience wears thin!'

Alice motioned him over to where she was stood. She motioned him to bend down that she wanted to whisper something in his ears. He didn't need to bend too far. I was shaking my head furiously at Alice who didn't seem to take any notice of me. Clive poked his ear forward towards Alice. I got myself ready to attack and protect my little sister if need be.

'And I said finders keepers, that's the rule,' Alice bellowed and she finished off by blowing a raspberry at the men again for the second time in a row.

Now not even I anticipated she would do that, such were the characteristics of my little sister Alice.

'Oh is it?'

He said still grinning as he used his finger to unblock his now half deaf ear. While his colleague was trying hard not to laugh, I could see him biting his thick lips, he would have needed to try harder because he was making a complete mess of it. Fat Clive snatched a hanky dangling from his colleague's pocket, dried his face then quickly tossed it back at him.

'I told you these kids are fooling around with us, they're hard as nails.'

'Sharapp! So you think it's nice to take something that doesn't belong to you, yeah?'

'We know what you're trying to do.'

'Yeah, you're trying to bully us into telling you where the map is but it's not going to work.'

'So you do know where the map is then?'

'Yeah, but we're not telling you and you don't scare us either, neither of you.'

'Is that so, well we'll soon see about that won't we Igor?'

'Clive, it's Ian, my name's Ian, remember?'

Clive slapped the palm of his right hand across his own forehead, he wasn't best pleased. I was because I now knew the names of both our assailants.

## Bio Fact

Name: Ian aka Igor
Age: unknown
Nickname: The silly one
Hobbies: Acting silly!
Most interesting fact: He can't help being silly!

'Now as I'm a kind-hearted man, a lover of kids especially bright kids like you lot so I'm going to ask you one more time and one time only. That map which you found hidden beneath one of those wooden floor boards, give it to me.'

'You didn't say please, 'Alice was kind to point out.

'Ok, pleaseeeeeeeeeeeee,' Clive retorted as he gritted his teeth like he was posing for a photograph.

'Why is the map so precious to you that you are prepared to do anything for it?'

Another nonsensical question from Alice likely to put us right in it yet again!

Just why did it not occur to Alice that maps are precious to anyone who actually needs one; I guess that's what makes them maps, they contain important information about how to get from one important place to another. The two men did what I had learnt to do all my life, ignore her.

What followed after that was a period of uncomfortable silence, a very long period something I thought would never happen. Even Alice kept her mouth shut. I avoided eye contact with the two men and I guess she also noticed this and did the same clever thing. They were waiting for us to respond and we were waiting for them to respond to our lack of response but it didn't happen.

'I'm guessing your answer is no then?'

We both exchanged glances then nodded in unison.

'As they always say, be prepared! To be prepared is to anticipate.'

Clive declared and then did the oddest thing. He revealed what he had underneath his arm, a camping chair, which he carefully unfolded, placed in the middle of the room then sat on it. He seemed to have anticipated a lot more because no sooner was Clive sitting comfortably, he clicked his finger. His colleague Igor responded by revealing what he had behind his back. It turned out to be a newspaper, a flask, some lumps of sugar concealed in a little plastic bowl along with a tea cup and saucer. He placed the items in front of stumpy Clive who then made himself a cup of tea and sipped it without a care in the world. Even though he was the one enjoying the luxury of a hot cup of tea, we were the ones sweating! Clive then removed a pair of spectacles from his top pocket which he perched on his nose, and began to read the newspaper.

'Surprised are you? Well we can do this all day, we're in no hurry. In fact, we have all the time in the world for you. As you can see we have come very prepared so whenever you're ready, in your own time of course you WILL tell me where my map is, I'm in no hurry at all.'

From where I was stood it looked like that for sure as he went back to his reading immediately after he spoke. And true to his words he seemed very relaxed and very unruffled.

'So what's important about finding this...'

'Alice!'

I screamed out so loud it must have been enough to wake her dead brain. When is enough ever enough for her I wondered.

'...oak tree?'

Alice was never going to give it up.

'Now we have been very patient, Alice, it is Alice isn't it?'

Alice was surprised that Clive referred to her by her actual name rather than young lady. I wondered why considering the fact that the way I had to scream her name half the town knows it too. Clive turned to his colleague for thumbs up but he was in a world of his own so he returned to the reading of his newspaper. 'I've even answered your millions of question so wherever you have hidden the map, get it, give it to me so we can go on our way and you can go on yours...did you just say oak tree before?'

What Alice had said like 10 hours ago had just registered in the fat man's mind.

'Still don't know the attraction to an oak tree,' Alice stuttered.

'Oak tree!' both men exclaimed.

'Well that is what you're looking for isn't it?' Alice again.

Both men exchanged glances at each other. Alice missed it but she did a lot of things. They nodded simultaneously but I was far from convinced.

'There is no oak tree,' I blurted out effortlessly.

'What?' Alice stared at me.

'I've studied the map, I've done my research, and I'm sure now there is no oak tree.'

'And you say you're sure about that?'

'I'm absolutely certain.'

'You mean we've been wasting our time all this while.'

I stared at Alice and she in return stared back at me. She had the so-I-was-right-and-you-were-wrong stare.

'I knew it,' Alice continued as she leapt into the air fists clenched, tongue out.

'Not quite, Alice, because I've discovered something, and it was that something I wanted to share with you…and before you go on with yourself, which I'm sure you're tempted to do, hear me out for what I have to say…'

WE WANT THE
MAP

hands →

← hands

# Chapter Eleven

## The Great Discovery

Both men glanced at each other then laughed a very horrible and wicked laugh. They laughed so loud and wide I could see right to the back of their mouths, their tonsils dangling about. It was not a pretty sight!

'You seem smarter than you look, boy,' Clive declared.

'Yeah, share with us your 'great discovery' genius,' Igor taunted.

'The oak tree, it doesn't exist but I guess that's no surprise to you both as you already knew that.'

Both men that were so into their laughter no longer found anything funny to laugh about!

'Clive and I don't know what you're taking about.'

'Really.'

Alice seemed very confused, she scratched her head.

'Well is there an oak tree or isn't there?'

'There isn't one but there used to be,' I continued.

'What?'

My last statement didn't make her any the less confused. I didn't blame her.

'The oak tree, it used to be the name of a popular local pub many, many years ago, before Mum and Dad's time, even before Granddad's and Grandma's time. For many years it had thrived using barley from the local farms around. As soon as business ventures started to make their way into the town, the pub could not compete; it ran out of business forcing it to close down. The building was abandoned for years, unused and left to rot. It was due to be demolished. This was until it was revived by a local business man and turned into a plausible venture so what lies there now…

'What is it?'

'A bank.'

'And you got this information from… let me guess, the internet?' Alice sarcastically bleated out loud.

'Precisely, and it's the same bank that Mum goes to get her cash when she goes on her weekly Saturday shopping spree.'

'I still don't get the connection. What's a bank got to do with a map?' Alice said.

'To be honest, I'm still trying to work it out…'

While Alice was having a go, I was thinking back to the history lesson and what interesting facts I had managed to learn. For someone who loathed history, I had done a great job to not fall asleep during any part of the lesson. Something I was yet to achieve since I became a student of the school!

C'mon think, Dan, think I challenged myself.

'That's it!' I screamed successfully scaring everyone as I pointed a finger into the air.

Clive jolted almost falling off his chair.

I was clearly having my light bulb flashing over my head moment and wasn't going to be denied.

'The map, those thick black squiggly lines, which we thought was a train track.'

'Yeah.'

'Well, it's not. It's a shaft; they are going to use the shaft.'

Remember it was in the history class that I had gotten into a heap of trouble but it seems every cloud had a silver lining and the class its worth.

'But how are you sure?'

'Mr Bonesworth, he mentioned it in history class and now it makes perfect sense.'

I could hear his exact words banging on the inside of my head; it was playing like I was watching a film.

'...so as a former mining town those many years ago the main stay commodity for the people was coal. As you well know, coal was the main source of power for the trains and also source of energy for the Nation at the time. People relied heavily on coal for cooking and heating during the winter. Now the coal would be dug up from the mines and the shafts used to transport the coal to places where it was easily assessable to be sold. These shafts obviously were known as coal shafts.'

I didn't mention everything he said as it would have bored them to death, I just keep the important words and got rid of the irrelevant ones, this is commonly known as paraphrasing!

'There's a shaft that runs underneath the town and stretches from one side of it to the other. When it was a pub the old shaft would have been handy to transport barrels of beer to the distribution centre saving costs. That explains why the pub lasted as long as it did and why it was able to sell cheap beer, it was easy to transport!'

'The shaft, but it's old and no longer accessible to the public.'

'Exactly, that's why if anyone uses it, who's going to know?'

'Clive,' Igor placed his hand on his back and gave it a gentle pat, 'let's give it to the kid, he is smart and…'

'Will you just shut up,' Clive bellowed as he snatched the offending hand off his back and flung it into the air.

'So what you're saying is that these two men are trying to rob the town's bank?'

'Yes.'

'Well, then that makes them both…'

'…Bank Robbers!' Alice and I let out a simultaneous loud shriek.

Both Clive and Igor looked at me like two hungry snarling wolves in pursuit of an innocent sheep.

'Great! They've…'

Clive leapt on Igor and muffled his voice with the palm of his dirty hand. He then looked at us with that horrible grin of his.

'Kids this story tale, fairy-tale or whatever you want to call it about us, I find very amusing and most intriguing but why on earth would we want to rob a bank?'

'We don't know.'

'And it's not for us to find out, that's a job for the police.'

'Yeah only slight problem is you're not going to the police now are you?'

He burst into laughter with the most annoying laugh which I wasn't used to, Alice was.

'Why can't they go, Clive, who's going to stop them?'

'We are of course, you idiot. Now grab them fool, tie them both up.'

'What with?'

Clive pretended to think hard.

'Uh, now let me see... well we have some rusty old nails over there, a couple of glass jars here, we also have scrap paper in the bin just there...'

'...don't forget this ancient looking axe here, look.'

'Get that thing out of my sight, idiot. What were you thinking of using to tie them up in the first place, something strong and reliable would be a nice start, don't you think?'

'Boss you're definitely the man with the brains around here.'

'Now quit jiving and do as you're told. So kids, are you going to tell me where the map is or shall we go all nasty on you, your choice...what are you going to do?'

Igor suddenly distracted him.

'What do you think you're doing?'

'Tying them up with string after all you did say try something strong and reliable.'

'Sometimes I wonder. GIVE ME THAT PACKET! Liquorice strings!'

'It cost me £1.99 for a pack of 10, it doesn't come cheap you know.'

'I don't believe this; you're tying the kids up with sweets. Have you lost your mind? You really think that's going to hold them down!'

'Oh maybe I should use their laces instead.'

'Yeah maybe you should, brainwave.'

While the drama was unfolding right in front of our very eyes, we sincerely had hoped we weren't the ones caught in the middle of it but as fate would have it, we were. Igor tied our hands and legs up till we were wrapped up like Christmas presents. Clive was delighted and clasped both his hands as if he wanted to pray. Alice and I were in dire need of some divine intervention of our own of some sort, of any sort. Suddenly, out of the blue there was a heavy banging on the door. Our prayers had been answered!

'Open up!' the voice bellowed.

'Are you expecting anyone?' Clive whispered to me. I shook my head.

'Open up I said, it's the police,' the deep voice continued.

'You idiot, I thought you said this place was safe?' Clive quizzed Igor.

'It is,' he whispered back.'

'Well obviously not or how else could they have found us?'

'The kids, they must have alerted them.'

'I said open the door or I'm breaking it down and I know someone is in there, I can hear you whispering,' the voice continued.

Both men who were now shaking like leaves.

'Okay then have it your way. Now I'll count to three and if you haven't decided to open this door I will break it down, one!

Clive and Igor were tripping over each other as they scampered around clearly not knowing what to do. The voice did!

'Two!'

'This is great, just great,' Clive lamented.

'Three!'

The men were about to charge through the front door when we all heard a long winding fart from outside.

'Eat that suckers…'

'What the…'

'Clive opened the door and bundled Ben in.'

'Alice, Dan.'

'Get in there you little joker.'

'Ben, what are you doing here?'

'I was looking for you guys, knew you'd be here.'

'Who else knows you're here kid?' Clive grunted.

'No one.'

'Excellent.'

'Who are these guys?'

'Oh they're robbers,' Alice replied nonchalantly.

'Robbers, as in… sorry guys I must have taken the wrong turn, see ya.'

'And where exactly do you think you're going?!' Igor blocked the doorway.

'Excellent, three for the price of two, well you can gladly join your friends'.

'I'll give it a miss thanks.'

'Oh but I insist.'

'Eh…'

A gentle shove from behind and Benji had joined us in a heap on the floor. He smiled at us with one of his false smiles. We didn't smile back, he knew why. Let's say it had to do with the fact that we could all have been free if not for yet another callous individual!

'Tie him up, too, Igor and with proper rope this time.'

'You keep forgetting my name its Ian not Igor.'

'I give up on you, I really do.'

'Who are you?' Benji spoke in a whisper.

'You can call me Uncle Clive and he's Dumbo without the big ears.'

'You've come at the right time.'

'OK, so now we're complete and aren't expecting any more guests, let's resume that game kids.'

'They're Robbers. They're planning to rob the town bank.'

I could hear Alice whisper in Benji's ears and so could the men. At least that cleared it up. We all now were in no doubt as to whom Clive and Igor were and what they were up to. Not that it made any difference to us as we couldn't do anything about it!

'Let's assume just this once that we are Bank robbers planning to rob a bank, just as clever clogs here has stated, which I must stress and make very clear that we are not, how do you think we would plan it?', Clive inquired.

'We aren't stupid you know. You plan to do it old school.'

'Old school, hmm now I'm intrigued. Have you ever tried to rob a bank in broad daylight with thousands of people passing by?'

'Yeah, are you mad? People will see us.'

'I never said you'd do it during the day though did I.'

'The shaft you're talking about ends by the Post Office; the bank is at least two buildings away. There is no way we can manage that.'

'Yeah unless you blast through the thick wall.'

'We will need something really powerful to do that.'

'This is unbelievable, how does he know we'll use Dyna...'

Once again Clive is told to shut up but it's too late.

'Dynamite but of course!'

'C'mon kids, dynamite, seriously. If we use dynamite, even the man on the moon will hear us.'

They were so right you know. The sound of dynamite would bring the police crawling in faster than they could say Jack Sparrow! So here I was the so called kid with the brains totally now at a complete crossroad.

'Not if it's on bonfire night!'

'BONFIRE NIGHT! That's it Alice, that's it, well done.'

Bonfire night was indeed on Friday that's when they planned to rob the bank.

'How are you so sure?'

'Mum, she always goes shopping on Saturdays, how else do you think she gets the money...cash machine. It always gets stocked up overnight for the weekend rush.'

'I give it to you, kids aren't stupid.'

'They're not, you are. Stop giving them hi fives and get to the ready.'

'So what happens now, you're just going to keep us here against our wishes?'

'Don't you worry yourself about that?'

'I'm not, you should be though.'

'And why should I.'

'Well, first of all, isn't there a law about keeping people against their wishes commonly known as kidnapping and secondly think about it. In a few hours' time when our parents don't see us, we will be declared missing and where do you think they will go.'

'Police.'

'Exactly.'

I was clearly calling their bluff and hoped it would work.

'My Dad won't, he's fearless.'

'Is he now?'

'Yeah, he's a fearless, six foot nine, eighteen stone wrestling tower of a man. If he finds out I'm missing, he will go crazy and no one likes it when my Dad goes crazy. His eyes go red, he gets the shakes, steam jets out of his nose like a raging bull. He will gorge your eyes out and rip your heads off piece by piece.

Benji's description of his Dad was believable until the part where he likened him to a raging bull and then that totally put us all off! We knew his Dad and he was nothing like that.

'Oh I'm very scared, aren't you?'

Igor was biting his finger nails nervously.

'I don't like the sound of his Dad one bit.'

'Oh be quiet. Can't you tell when kids are having you on?'

'Our Parents, they'll piece everything together, in your case maybe not, they will surely trace us to this place, they will find us and for you it will be game over.'

'You mean like wreck it, Ralph, game over?'

'Will you just shut up?'

'Maybe we should reconsider.'

Clive thought s hard for a long while. 'You know what; get out of their way Igor, Untie them, open the door, let them go.'

'Really!'

'You heard what I said. Get out of the kids way, open the door and let them go.'

Igor obliged by untying us and opening the door. The sight of the sky and the trees and everything else was heaven, and so was the sweet thought of freedom, it looked like my plan had worked after all!

'Kids, you're free to go.'

'Seriously, because we're going straight to the police right now.'

'Yeah, you're not getting away with this and we're telling them of your evil plan.'

'What's so funny because we meant every word just now?'

'I don't think you have any reason to laugh.'

'Well I can at least think of three.' Clive was still smirking.

He pointed to each of us in turn.

'You'll be laughing all the way to prison when we tell the Police what you're up to.'

'Tell them.'

'We'll show them the map.'

'Show them but I would take a good look at it before you do.'

Yeah, like we'd fall for that old chestnut! He would tease us enough to produce the map which he would then snatch off us and in a flash there would go the evidence. Like Clive said himself, we were kids, but not stupid ones!

'Do you think they'll take you seriously? Have you seen the map? It looks like a drawing from a three year old's scrap book.'

'Eh I drew the map, Clive.'

'Exactly.'

'It's a trick.'

'Do it.'

If he was calling our bluff, he was doing a good job of it.

'I said go ahead and do it.'

'What are you doing egging them on, are you mad boss.'

'Think about it you fool. Who will listen to a bunch of kids going on about an imaginary map? A map they probably don't have by now anyway. They do it all the time. No-on will take them serious, no big deal over a stupid map.'

'Boss you're the greatest.'

'They don't call me brains for nothing.'

'You're right, not unless of course our little conversation is recorded. You see, it takes more than that to outfox kids especially with brains like ours.'

'What!'

'Mobile phones are very handy gadgets these days; they can do anything and everything.'

I produce my iPhone from out of my pocket in a flash. At the press of a button I play back a snippet of our conversation and every word spoken was as clear as day including their boast of the pending heist.

'Don't just stand there muttering to yourself Clive, grab the mobile.'

'Give me that.'

Igor rudely snatched it out of my grasp before I even had time to think.

'Your right to freedom has just been revoked.'

I was right to declare how crafty I had been but why oh why didn't I do that after we had left the shed and not before? Clive slammed the door shut and both men re-formed the two man barricade around us. I realised at that moment I was becoming like Alice not knowing when to keep my mouth shut!

The two men cowed over us shadow and all and edged slowly towards us as we edged swiftly away from them. We soon found ourselves cornered into the shed wall with nowhere else to go. Yes we were truly and utterly stumped and all conclusions lead to the fact that now we were well and truly...

Dan's Dad

# Chapter Twelve

## Trapped!

Clive who had managed to snatch my iPhone off me somehow deleted the recording that I had made along with some of my long life memories. He placed the phone on the table and made it clear that any funny business would reduce my cherished asset into mere scrap by the time he was finished with it. I wasn't a popular figure in the eyes of neither Alice nor Benji. Their constant glances and gnarly looks at my direction confirmed this, yet I had the nerve to refer to Alice as the one who'd say things before actually thinking first about what to say!

'Clive, tie them up again. They look innocent but I don't trust them anymore. This time it's for real and WE WILL make them talk.'

Igor walked sluggishly towards us.

'Get out of my way; I'll tie them up myself. There you are. Now as you can see I have tied your hands in the front and not the back. We don't want your delicate hands dropping off do we, well not yet anyway?'

Alice had been clutching hard to her doll throughout the mayhem, she was still holding tight to it but had since let go of the comb.

'I want that map,' Clive bellowed.

We did not say anything, no one moved a muscle. After what seemed like ages of us all just constantly eyeballing each other, Clive decided to break the ice.

'Well, I guess you kids need some time to get your thoughts together, I understand that, but all that hard thinking does make you hungry. I think it's time for some lunch, don't you?'

'Right, you are boss.'

Igor snatched the handkerchief from his pocket. The same one that Clive used to clean his face; lazily he tucked it into his shirt collar creating a makeshift napkin. Then he produced several food items including an object wrapped in cellophane. Carefully he unwrapped it to reveal a rolled up buttie. He opened his mouth so wide that we could see all his horrible crocked teeth. Clive turned round just as he was about to take the first bite.

'What on earth are you doing?'

'Having me lunch.'

'Not you, I was referring to the kids, nitwit.'

'Oh right. Well kids, what have we got here, let's see, you'll have to make do with sausage roll...

'Give me that,' he whacked it out of his outstretched hands.

'Eww! They're not going to eat your soggy rolls, dumb head, they're kids, they don't eat that rubbish. Go get them a proper meal like fries and chicken nuggets. Anyone for some lunch, my treat?'

I knew we were all starving but none of us moved, no one wanted to expose their weakness.

'Anyway, Igor will go and get us some lunch.'

'I will?'

'Oh yeah you will. Get down to the local eatery and get the kids' burger, chips, milkshake the works, get me my regular and you get yourself what you want and make it snappy, never keep hungry kids waiting! Now go.'

Igor had hardly opened the door when Clive shoved him out. The silent waiting game continued until Igor returned with bags of food which he distributed amongst us despite our protests that we weren't hungry and that the food stank. Clive requested sarcastically that we eat, I noticed Alice was about to decline with a typical raspberry blow, I could see her mouth beginning to shape up, I quickly jumped in.

'Ok, we'll eat since you insist but don't think this will make us say any more than we have already because we won't right, Benji?'

'Right!'

'Right Alice?'

'Right.'

Phew, I had brought us some precious time, talk about being as cunning as a fox! As we tucked into the meal, it just occurred to me that the goblin figurine neatly wrapped amongst the fries would complete my whole goblin collection. It should have been a cause for celebration considering the fact that I now had a chance to win tickets to see Slime live in concert, but obviously it wasn't! Alice was eating as if she had all the time in the world. She was always a slow eater but today she seemed mega slow and disinterested. She was chewing at her fries as if they were gum and cautiously sucking at her milkshake as if it was sure to make her ill. Benji on the other hand was almost eating through the paper wrappings as he slurped away at his drink. Strange actions from kids who had earlier declared they were NOT hungry. Benji hid that very well! I was eating under the influence of my deep thoughts. Even the taste of the burger and fries wasn't enough to dissuade me. All the while I was thinking of a plan, to escape and everything else was a smokescreen but in order for this to be achieved I needed other things to go my way, I was hoping and praying that it did and pretty soon…

The longer the minutes rolled by since we had been apprehended by these worthless two and held hostage in our little shed over a silly map, the longer it seemed before someone had a word to say. No guesses as to who that someone turned out to be!

'How long do you actually plan to keep us here?''

The answer to the foolish question was very simple, as long as they wanted.

The two men laughed long and hard and very loud, and understandably so. I mean, had it not occurred to Alice (because it had certainly occurred to me) that this hut would be the last place any of our parents would be likely to search for us, for one very good reason, they don't know this place exists. I guess that was why we proudly displaced the 'secret location' sign we had unwittingly left hanging over the makeshift mantelpiece duh. Another classic example of Alice talking first and then thinking!

'So what happens now?'

'Kids, you're our guests. Have your tea first and then you'll see,' Clive smirked.

'I'm not hungry,' Alice declared defiantly.

This was obvious by the way she was mashing the fries into different weird shapes as if it was play doh.

'Do you like pets?'

'I love fish, especially goldfish, I think they're cute.'

'Shut up, I was referring to the kids not you, Igor.'

'I've got two goldfish, Perky and Rambo; had them since I was five years old.'

'Perky and Rambo, they sound like stowaway fishes.'

I for one did not take kindly to the insult rained on my poor, harmless fishes.

'How about dogs, do you like dogs?'

Before I could speak guess who interjected!

'I hate dogs and I find them despicable creatures,' Alice screamed as she annoyingly spat out a chip that fell next to Clive's' boot.

He looked at Alice as if he wanted to say something but stopped himself. He walked over to where the discarded chip was, raised his boot high in the air and landed on it with a splatter. Clive grinned menacingly. Igor had meanwhile started to distribute the crayons he had brought along with some sheets of paper amongst us. I guess it was their way of buying time as the interrogation of the whereabouts of the map would continue. I failed to tell you that Alice had a knack for art. So while Benji decided to nervously bite into his crayons until there was a tiny heap of crayon mess, I used mine to create a meaningless diagram. Alice, on the other hand was putting all this time we had at our disposal to sketch out a picture. It didn't take long for me to identify exactly what she was drawing, a picture of the old bee hive. Why she did that only she would ever know, she just did and it was just as hideous as the real life one!

'Excellent, Igor, now get Bruiser, He'll make them talk.'

'Right you are Boss.'

Clive assured us that the legend of the Loch Ness Monster would be nothing compared to the harrowing experience we would be exposed to by Bruiser. It didn't move me one bit but again, I only spoke for myself!

'Who's Bruiser?' Alice said with a quaver in her voice.

'Don't worry, dear, you'll soon find out.'

As Igor left the hut, that of course was our worry. He soon returned but empty-handed.

'Where is he?'

'What do you mean where is he?'

'For goodness sake, do I have to handle everything myself.'

The two men disappeared out of the shed presenting me with the opportunity I was looking for and which had now arrived. I needed to take full advantage and quick. I got up as fast as I could, considering the fact that I had been strapped up like a mummy I was quite nippy, and hobbled over to where my phone had been left. Plan A was well and truly in full swing.

Door firmly secured

# Chapter Thirteen

## Plan A

If there was anything closer to my heart than football, science and my best pal Benji, then it had to be my phone. Once upon a time when my parents were human (exactly a year ago) believe it or not, but they bought me an iPhone for my birthday. It was like my second heartbeat. I would take it everywhere and anywhere. School, the library, church, it never left my sight. I knew it inside out, back to front. The time I invested on the phone meant I could work it blindfolded. This would eventually come in handy considering the fact that I had been deprived full use of my hands and legs. The phone was perfect for everything I needed in a phone. I mean it had a camera, calculator, and the recording machine that got me into trouble! It had various useful apps but best of all it was a phone, the best thing it could be right now!

I managed to somehow grab it and press a number on the key pad with my nose. Something that I had never done before and thought I could never do successfully until now. My phone was just awesome. It had a facility which was voice activated so I only needed to say the name I wanted to dial and it would do exactly that.

'There's only 1 signal bar on the phone. I don't know if it will work though,' I declared trying not to sound downbeat.

'Just try it and hurry; they'll be back any second now,' I could hear the panic in Benji's voice.

Maybe it was the signal but after a few frantic attempts, it finally dialled 'Dad' having searched for 'bad' and a host of other close call options. Anyway the phone started to ring…

'Here goes, hey the phone's ringing!'

'… Philip Chambers speaking.'

'Dad, it's me.'

'Is that Daniel?'

'Yeah.'

'Now why am I not surprised, Daniel. What do you want?'

'I've got to make this quick.'

'And why are you whispering. Let me guess, you're whispering because you're in the middle of a class making sneaky phone calls when really you shouldn't be. You should be paying attention to your Teacher.'

'No, I mean yes, but we've been kidnapped by two robbers.'

'You're playing cops and robbers. Now why do you think I need to know that in the middle of a very important business meeting, Daniel Jeremiah Chambers?'

'No Dad, we're trapped in a hut by two robbers.'

'You have still not got my message have you? There goes your pocket money for a week.'

'Dad…

'I'll make that two weeks if you don't hang up and I will deal with you when I get home and don't call me again as I am very busy unlike some people.'

'No Dad wait…'

'What did he say,' Benji stared at me with his wide eyes expectant of good news.

'He hung up. He didn't hear a word,' I said, but I heard every word he said, something tells me I'm in trouble, again!'

'Call 999.'

'Great idea.'

'Na bad idea. Hand it over.'

Clive snatched the phone off me and having warned me that any bad behaviour he would smash it up, he did just that.

'Noooooooooooo!' I screamed.

Meanwhile Ian walked in carrying a bag he was struggling to hold on to. He knelt to the ground and carefully opened it. Out popped a Chihuahua whom the men commanded to 'get.'

The tiny dog stared at us and then began to sniff at the ground.

'Is that Bruiser?' I enquired to know as I pointed at the diminutive sight in front of me.

Igor nodded confidently.

Despite the loss of my prized asset, my disappointment was soon forgotten by this latest drama. I tried hard to bite my lip to stop myself, it didn't work. I burst into this crazy, uncontrollable and most annoying laugh (take a bow Alice).I surprised even myself. I didn't know where it came from, it just did. I laughed so hard and so loud my ribs began to hurt.

'Oh you think it's funny do you, well watch this!'

Igor grabbed Alice's doll and waved it in the face of the Chihuahua.

A cute Bruiser

'What are you doing?' Alice demanded.

Whatever it was he was doing, it seemed to spark the dog to life. It snarled at Bessie then to our utmost horror snatched the doll out of the man's grasp, her head popped off immediately. You would have thought it would stop there, let her go? But oh no, poor old Bessie had it coming. Bruiser snarled wildly, tongue out, teeth gnashing, eyes rolling as he flung her to the left and then to the right, up and then down before spinning round and round twisting and turning as he did. And all this while he had Bessie clasped in between his sharp teeth refusing to let her go. I was watching Alice through the corner of my eye. She was trying hard to catch up with the dog's swift movement but with very little success. When Bruiser was done having the time of its life, it spat Bessie to the ground, at least what was left of her, which I must say was very, very little. At this point I could barely look at Alice's face. I always threatened that I would one day take Bessie's head off and chuck her in the bin but I never ever even meant it, it was always going to be an empty threat (not that I had ever told Alice though). Both Ben and I were stunned to silence staring at Alice awaiting her reaction as Clive handed Bessie back to her – her one time superstar doll, a doll she owned since the age of two –piece by piece. He smirked as he did the honours.

'Oh no you didn't.'

'Oh yes I did.'

'Noooooooooooooooo!'

In a flash of the moment and like something only a blockbuster movie could provide, Alice suddenly found super strength from only God knows where and snatched away the laces on her hands as if they were thread. She leapt up onto her feet (though they were also tied) and as Clive advanced swiftly towards her she flung him over her shoulder. He crashed to the ground. I could see tiny stars circle around his head.

'Hey you little…'

Alice snatched Igor's arm from off her shoulder and threw him into the air. He joined Clive in a heap on the floor

'Wow Alice!' Benji squelched in delight.

'Alice, where did that come from?' I enquired.

'You know those lessons that I take after school every Wednesdays that you call soppy – it's called karate lessons.'

'Oh.'

'So what do we do know?' Benji asked.

Well we had plan A and that had failed, we had no plan B. So when faced with a situation such as this, there was really only one thing left to do.

Alice, Benji and I exchanged glances at one another.

'Run!' we all screamed together.

An angry Bruiser

# Chapter Fourteen

## The Great Escape

We bolted out of the shed as fast as our legs could carry us. The fresh air couldn't have smelt any better.

'Wait, I've forgotten something important, I've got to go back.'

'What's so important that you'd risk your life?'

That question was answered a couple of minutes later when I re-emerged holding the leftover of my phone whilst clutching my trouser pocket. Isn't it great that in times like these we are faced with several choices something that we lacked seconds or so ago! Well, we had the choice of splitting up so each person would take separate paths, or two of us go together and one alone. The compass on my phone would have come in handy for this moment but that wasn't to be.

'There they are!'

We choose neither, we bundled ourselves quickly on the first path we could find.

'Head that way quick…'

'That way' led us to a foot path which in turn led to a muddy field. We barely had the nerve to look back but when I did, I noticed the two men were quickly gaining on us. Trudging through the mucky fields was slowing them down but they weren't the only ones affected.

'My shoe's slipping off, I can feel it.'

'Keep going, Benji, we're almost there.'

As if I knew where 'there' was! Anyway, we meandered our way and quickly ended up at the edge of a little brook. We tiptoed though the jagged rocks to the other side arriving at the comfort of even more bushes. We wasted no time diving into the thicket and trudged for as far as our tired legs could take us. I motioned that we all remain silent and dare not move a muscle. Benji was bright red in the face so much so, I thought he was going to explode any moment now. Alice was trying her best not to sob.

'Don't say a word,' I whispered.

'I want Mum,' Alice declared.

'I just want to go home,' Benji whispered back.

I felt sorry for Alice, she didn't have a doll to cuddle no more, I felt sorry for Benji. I knew what they wanted but I couldn't deliver either.

'C'mon kids do we have to do this, seriously.'

We could hear Clive's voice.

'Ouch, I think I just touched a nettle.'

And Igor's!

It was obvious they were quickly gaining on us and we hadn't gone far enough. So I motioned for one final heave from us all and one final heave was exactly what I got because after that, eventually we could go no further.

We had maintained our crouching positions for quite a while of which during this period we had heard nothing. I didn't know whether to see it as a good omen or terrifying one. But before I or anyone else could gather our thoughts together, we began to hear a faint rustling of leaves. I motioned again for them to follow my lead as I crouched down as low to the ground as I could. Soon all three of us had assumed a most awkward huddle. The rustling was getting louder and louder still. Suddenly, it stopped! By now the rate of our heartbeats pounding against our chest was going into overdrive. I couldn't bear to think of the unthinkable. Surely we were doomed!

'Oy!'

I felt a hand over my shoulder, forget being brave, I wanted to scream to the end of the earth. I could barely look up.

'Daniel.'

I plucked up courage to look up, Alice couldn't and neither could Ben. Bearing down at me, beaming with a smile was a female police officer. I had never been happier to see a uniformed member of the people's protection force.

'Daniel Chambers?'

'Yes,' I replied feebly.

'…are you okay?'

I nodded then quickly shook both Alice and Ben who were still crouching with their faces pressed to the ground

'Guys, they are over here,' she shouted out.

The police woman stretched her hand forward towards me and I grabbed it without any further questions asked. She dragged me from the thicket and one by one she pulled us all out until with were safely stood out on the open road. We were soon surrounded by more Police officers asking us if were okay. Besides the fact that Alice no longer had her Superstar doll Bessie, the only tragedy to report, we were all fine, visibly shaken, but fine. I had noticed Dad's and Mum's car parked in the corner by a tree. No sooner had I spotted it than they both appeared from no-where, their faces were filled with panic. Dad had the added guilt on his face; I hoped that after this experience, maybe just maybe this time I could be someone he could rely on for once. I was waiting for an apology, as Dad stood in front of me observing this weird silence. He then just picked me up in his arms shook me as if I myself was a doll then gave me the biggest hug ever. Okay, apology accepted I guess. Mum soon snatched me away and with tears in her eyes embraced Alice and I. By now I could also see Benji's parents arrive. His mum dashed past the Police and held her son aloft as if he were a trophy. She ladened him with kisses as she also drenched him in tears while his Dad almost gorged his eyes out whilst checking them to see if he was still alive!

'I'm sorry about Bessie,' I whispered to Alice as soon as I was able to get my breath back.

'Don't be stupid.'

'I didn't really realise how much she meant to you till today.'

'She didn't matter to me that much, I guess there are more important things in life.'

Alice looked into Benji's direction and very swiftly into mine as she spoke.

'Besides,' she continued,' I was getting far too old for her anyway, I'm a big girl now. Normally I'd quickly remind her that I was the bigger one being the oldest and she the smaller one being the youngest, I didn't need to be told, so for once I decided to let it slide, something she really deserved!

'I'm really happy you're my sister you know. Little sister maybe,' I smiled back.

Sorry, I just had to get it in there!

'You don't have to be nice to me.'

'I need you to know that because sometimes neither my words nor actions say enough.

'Say that again, but louder', Alice cheekily requested.'

'No.'

'You mean to say that you really love me, don't you.'

'Don't push it, Alice.'

'Well thanks, it's nice to know. I'll always keep her close to my heart, Bessie.'

At that point the Police were escorting two very ragged looking criminals to a waiting police van. Clive was still rubbing his head while his partner was clutching his stomach. Both men were still quite r dazed. I guessed they had taken the wrong turn whilst they were pursuing us and ended up in the thorn bushes. This was confirmed to us later on! No sooner were they bundled into the car, it sped off to the chorus of sirens.

One of the policemen came forward; he looked like a very important figure.

'I'm Brian Watts, the town's Chief Constable,'

He shook the hands of the Dads very briskly but firmly. I thought Dad's hand was going to drop off.

'What a bunch of brave kids you have here, are you all okay?'

'We're fine but could do with a hot bath I guess.'

Benji seemed to have spoken on behalf of us all as we put aside our travails and joined in the merry laugh.

'What you did today, make no mistake about it, was highly courageous and worthy of everyone's praise. Those two criminals have been on our radar for years, they had given us the slip more times than a banana.'

From the way the adults were laughing, it was clear the Police Inspector was trying to make light of the severity of the situation so again we just went with it!

'Who's the leader amongst you kids?'

Both Benji and Alice immediately pointed in my direction then seemed to drag me slightly forward which I felt was very modest of them but at the same time very true!

'And you are Daniel.'

'Yes, sir.'

'So then you must be Benji.'

'Yes, sir.'

He pointed to each of us in turn.

'And you definitely must be Alice.'

'Yes, sir.'

You can drop the sir; I get called that all the time. It's nice to be called by my actually name, so you can all call me Brian

'Yes, sir, Brian, sir,' we all chorused.

At least we tried!

Well, to be able to galvanise your troops in the mist of adversity gets my bravery vote any day of the week, we'll be in touch with each of your Parents regards what's gone on today but for now, let's take a trip down to the station there's some ice cream awaiting you all.

Well, let's just say I loved the sound of that and I wasn't the only one. Both Alice and Benji were already salivating on the thought.

At the police station we were given books to write the account of what had happened, which was what Benji and I did. Alice (being different), she just sketched hers out I guess it would come handy after all!

We were also introduced to a Man by the name Alan Proctor; he was the editor of the town's weekly newspaper. It was he who would take our stories away to be printed in the next publication. He promised to make it out as dramatic as the accounts of our stories had turned out to be!

'Watch out for your story in the next edition. There was a debate over what the title would turn out to be. We wanted it to be called 'The Shed'. Mr Proctor wasn't convinced that it would, in his words 'encapsulate your whole experience'. So eventually, we came up with the story conveniently titled 'The Bee Hive'. It had already started to sound very dramatic but I guess it had to be, and we, for one, weren't complaining. We actually loved the title better as it would be appropriate for our Hollywood blockbuster movie of the same title. Oh yes, we were thinking that far.

Soon after that we were served the ice cream as promised. It was well worth the wait. I had never seen a bigger sundae in my entire life wow! We all had the crunch mountain flavour served with crunchy pieces of chocolate fudge settled at the bottom of the glass. There were fluffy marshmallows placed in the middle and ice cream at the top with a generous topping of cream with chocolate cream oozing down it. If ever my dream of being a scientist wasn't to work out, this is what I would like to be right here, owner of the biggest ice cream shop the world would have to offer. I would have customers queuing at my shop from all corners of the world, Asia, Africa, North and South America, Australia. I'd be richer than the richest man and more famous than the Queen herself!

The bushes were our refuge

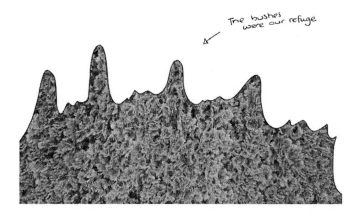

# Chapter Fifteen

## A Hero's Welcome

The mayor stood beaming with such a broad smile you would have though he had just hit the jackpot. To be frank if his immaculate set of white teeth gleamed any brighter, the photographers would no longer have any use for a flash! He stood proud as a peacock as he squeezed all three of us warmly. In a twinkle of an eye, we were surrounded by the several photographers who were like leaches feasting on a leaf as they jostled to get the best snaps for the daily papers and nations countless magazines. We were just content in trying to stay alive at least for the grand presentation! The television camera crew were also in attendance. We could see them drag our Parents about like rag dolls sticking microphones in front of them like carrots in front of horses as they thirst for more information about the towns new 'heroes'. The whole town was there and I mean literally the whole town was there!

The scene before our very eyes was incredible, it was magnificent, and we were lost for words.

Once the photoshoot was over and all interviews done, we were ushered to our seats on an excellently created platform situated slightly high up from the ground. We had an eagle's view of everyone.

From where I was sat, I could see famous footballers, actors and actresses, even politicians, they had all turned out just to see us and we were all so highly honoured. We weren't so enthusiastic about the three piece suit with bow tie that we were compelled to wear. Alice was wearing her beautiful flower girls dress that she had worn to Uncle Ste and Auntie Sally's wedding last year, so you could forgive us if you thought that was where we were all heading! The awkwardness of our dressing was soon forgotten by the appearance of a gigantic cake that had three action figures of us chasing two crooks. This was courtesy of all the townspeople in appreciation of what we had done. It bought a tear to my eye, the fact that such a most beautiful cake would eventually have to be devoured!

Across the street from where we sat, we could see a neatly and well decorated giant float embellished with our names and pictures, cheesy smile and all. On each side ran the words 'A hero's welcome for OUR heroes'. If it had been written any bigger, there would have been no space for our faces to appear! We would soon be situated on this incredible mobile float, specially created only for this grand occasion to be given the best seats in the house. We would be expected to travel each corner of the town waving to the jeering crowd in celebration of our exploits. That of course would follow but only after the Mayor's short speech.

He would start off by telling the world the history of this 'little town'. Nothing was spared. I mean he went on about the mining significance of the town and the role it played in the development of the other adjoining towns.

It was like Mr Bonesworth's history class all over again. It took him a full hour and could actually have taking much longer. His voice was disrupted by a slight technical hitch as the Mayor's microphone started to malfunction until it came to a complete stop. Rumour would have it that some concerned townsperson had eventually lost the will to live and seized an opportunity to sabotage the situation and cut the majestic Mayor's speech off. If anything, it would be a sign to our Mayor to get things moving a lot quicker as several heads were already drooping. We had all heard the story over and over again and just wanted to get the real reason why the world had actually stopped in honour of our darling town.

'Ladies and Gentlemen, boys and girls of our wonderful town…'

It was the Mayor's voice again. He apologised for the unplanned interval and seemed set to continue his boring speech. I thought I had heard the last from him, didn't we all. The last time he declared to speak, he promised it would be short and sweet and it turned out to be neither!

One of the officials quickly got up and whispered into his ear, to which he nodded and then pointed to the float

'Our heroes would like to meet their people.'

The Mayor's utterance was preceded by an explosive cheer from the crowd as we were escorted to our place on the float and once we were settled in, parents, delegates and all, we were off! I mean, I could have done that all day long, wave to the crowd as they threw flowers and tonnes of sweets at us, acknowledge people carrying posters and banners bearing our names and pictures of us we never even knew existed but for the minor fact that I was absolutely starving. I helped myself to the millions of sweets and chocolate bars scattered on the floor of the float. Such a great day was threatening to be completely ruined as I noticed the Mayor reaching out for a micro phone. He banged it lightly on his other arm and then blew into it producing a horrible screeching sound. What on earth was he about to say now that he hadn't already said, I wondered. I mean, the mayor had earlier presented us and our parents an envelope containing an all-expenses paid two week trip to Disney world Florida, and he made sure the pressmen and camera crew captured it all!

The float soon grounded to a halt.

'Ladies and Gentlemen, boys and girls of our wonderful town. I would like to show my gratitude on behalf of you these wonderful people to our three children here. To show our gratitude to you from the people of your loving township, for your heroics,' the Mayor spoke with a grin that seemed to be forever stuck to his face Here we go, I thought.

'I will grant all three of you your heart's desire. Ask for whatever it is that you want and consider it done.'

'What and you'll do it?' Alice enquired as she almost swallowed the microphone all in one.

'Preciously.'

'Anything?' Benji asked.

'Absolutely,' the Mayor replied.

As the Mayor placed the microphone to our mouths waiting for who would declare their wish first. I tried to comprehend what I had just heard the Mayor say and whether this was real life or one of those very long dreams. I couldn't believe what I had just heard and I was loving every bit of it just as much as I knew Alice and Benji were.

'Is this for real?'

The Mayor nodded gleefully as he appeared to read my mind.

Benji requested for a year's supply of McDonalds despite a clever attempt of a clip around the ear hole from his doting Dad for ignoring his whispers to choose wisely though Benji would argue that he did! Alice asked for a blank cheque to visit Superstar world and buy whatever she wanted, both were granted by our town's Mayor whose chest was puffed out looking on as proud as a peacock.

'And Daniel, what would you like?' the Mayor teased.

'Mine is easy; I don't even need to think,' my voice bellowed through the microphone. It was music to the ears of thousands of towns' people who had streamed out to grace the monumental occasion...

'Two front row tickets to the Slime concert,' Dad said in disgust as he drove us home.

'What a silly thing to ask for.'

'Shut up, Alice,' I demanded.

'Mum, Daniel told me to shut up.'

'Daniel!'

'Well, I wasn't talking to her was I? And don't get me started, Alice; I'm not in the mood.'

But clearly SHE was! Alice pulled her tongue at me, something I was more than used to. She kept her tongue hanging out of her mouth like a lizard, something I clearly wasn't!

'Stop pulling your tongue at me!' I said in disgust as I pointed into Alice's direction and at the same time Dad's.

'At least someone's got common sense.'

Alice was obviously referring to herself, another indication of how far she was prepared to go to wind me up!

'It was a good thing the Mayor was kind enough for you to go home, sleep over your request and really have a think about it.'

'I had thought about it.'

'Well your Dad and I don't think so.'

'Yeah, neither do I.'

'Alice, s-h-u-t u-p!'

'Mum, Dan just told me to shut up.'

'It's a lifetime request, Dan, and you want to get it right.'

'What's wrong with you kids these days eh? A year's supply of McDonalds!'

'Told you; the girls are the sensible ones and boys have the empty heads. How sensible was my request?'

I didn't respond to the insult or in fact anything else as I stared through the car window gazing at nothing in particular wondering how my life had ended up this way. I mean the year had started brightly enough for me. Then it rapidly went into decline before things began to suddenly look up for me with my hero status. Some hero status that had turned out to be! So there it was, the year would end on such a devastating note. That cloud with a silver lining was now confirmed to be completely vanished, utterly ruined by this latest demeanour. Thinking back now I should have wished for the ability to disappear from the face of the earth only to reappear as Rambo in a fish bowl without a care in the world! So there I was sulking all the way home. I had hoped that somehow my parents would get the message, turn the car round and head back to the Mayor's office to confirm my one and only request, some hope!

The mayor of the town beaming with glee.

# Chapter Sixteen

## A Christmas Day

Just like any other kid, I was looking forward to Xmas, this year was different. It was not for the excitement of unwrapping the 'lovely,' 'guess-what-I-got-for-Xmas' presents that Santa Claus nor anyone else was destined to provide but for one very important reason that to both my parents relief was not all about me! I determined to be the bigger person and be that man, even if it was just for a day. Somehow I managed to derive mental strength, don't ask me how, to put solidly behind me the drama of the past couple of weeks and of how my parents had scuppered my one and only chance on this entire earth to see Slime live in the land down under. It would have been an absolute and monumental dream come true for me now turned to nothing short of a disaster. I mean my whole family would have benefited in some shape or form from the kind gesture of the towns people and its Mayor if it had happened. So there, I had seen it all, what more could possibly go wrong in my young tender life that hadn't already!

So I was least surprised when the only present under the Xmas tree marked 'with love from Santa Claus' appeared to have the name Alice clearly written on it neatly wrapped with a beautiful pink ribbon tied around it. Alice smiled proudly as she carefully removed the ribbon and unwrapped the gift. I knew exactly what she was thinking, that I was the scum of the earth and rightly got nothing from Santa and she was the all-time princess that deserved everything from Santa. She took her time unwrapping the gift with the utmost care trying her best to limit the damage on this well designed present. It was clear it had been very carefully put together by Father Xmas. As she slowly did this making sure that my eyeballs followed her every step of the way, each piece of the wrapping paper she unfolded was supposed to cause me pain but far from it. I must have surprised everyone as rather than gape in awe, I was amazingly calm and collected.

'I guess every GOOD child deserves a well-earned present from the man himself,' Alice declared empathising on the word good whilst having a pop at me for the obvious reason that unlike her, I had not been deserving of a gift from St Nicolas.

'I will most definitely be the talk of town, the main attraction, the…'

Alice, suddenly speechless, surrounded by discarded wrapping paper had finally unwrapped the gift. Her eyes lit up as she stared into the box amazed at what was in front of her. It would soon be evident that she wouldn't be the only one surprised.

'Alice what have you got?'

She was too far gone in her trance to hear Mum blabbering on. Her eyes were lit up like Charlie when he found one of Willy Wonka's golden tickets. She placed both hands in the box and removed the object carefully placing it on the table before our very eyes.

'I don't believe this.'

'Bessie!'

No word of a lie. As there in the glare of us all, clothed in the most beautiful pink flowing dress looking as good as new, well almost, was indeed Bessie. Mum and Dad were puzzled.

'Who would do such a thing?'

Alice looked straight at me. She had clearly done the maths.

'Did you…it was you.'

'I don't know what you're on about' I quickly interjected.

'But someone must have…'

It just occurred to her that my going back to the shed that day was for one thing and one thing only and it wasn't to get my phone back.

'You went back to get Alice and not your phone'

'Don't be stupid Alice, I detested her remember. Why would I do such a thing?'

'I remember now, that's why you kept clutching at your trouser pocket. You didn't want me to see her.'

'You're talking rubbish Alice, I lost my belt, and my trousers kept falling down.'

'No, Dan, it was you, you did this.'

'Daniel, is it true?'

'You kept her all this time just to get her repaired?'

I always was a rotten liar; I couldn't even look anyone in the face without flinching.

'It must have cost you quite a lot of your pocket money.'

Actually, it cost me all my pocket money for the entire year AND extras just to get the best craftsman in the town to repair her to be exact, and it did not come cheap but yeah, I'm not complaining though.

'You did that for me?'

'Dan, you did that for your sister?'

I mumbled a few sentences in a language that neither I nor anyone else could understand. What I was trying to say was yeah, yeah, whatever, get over it, and just don't tell anyone in school what I did for you especially the lads on the football team. I was resisting the temptation to blush amidst all the praises that I was getting but I failed.

'That is the sweetest thing ever.'

The image of my sister giving me a smacker on my cheek would probably haunt me for the rest of my childhood and entire adult life but I guess with everything I had gone through and what she did for me , I could live with that! Despite her big mouth, pokey nose and all the rest of it, I loved me little sister with all my heart and that was never ever going to change. I can't believe I just told you that!

**MWAH**

# Chapter Seventeen

## All's Well…

Weeks had gone by since the whole town declared that we were no ordinary kids. Xmas had waved goodbye and with all the pent up drama of another year about to evaporate into the thinnest of air, we could all get back to living our normal lives again. So for me, the arrival of Saturday confirmed it was another match day and I had to get up ready in time to put my pride on the line for the love of my local football club and that was always gonna be a task and a half!

The night before I was stuck by an unusual illness of which I had declared could jeopardise my featuring at all during any part of the match. By the next morning I noticed my discarded football kit had been neatly packed by my room door confirming my parents had correctly guessed I would do anything to avoid playing in the blistering conditions even if it did mean feigning sickness!

'If we can brace the so called 'blistering' conditions just to watch you, then I see no reason why you can't make the effort to go out there and play.'

I could hear Dad break out into a song from a well know tune.

'What sad group of people would be out kicking a silly ball about on New Year's Day, besides me,' I requested to know but got no answer.

So since it was now clear I had the luxury of Mum's and Dad's company forced upon me, I had decided to make the effort and not be late! And everything was going according to plan until the doorbell rang!

'Dan, the doorbell's ringing which normally means there's someone's at the door,' Mum called out to me.

'Alice, get the door,' I bellowed to my sister.

'Get it yourself, lazy pig,' she bellowed back.

'Mum, Dad, Alice won't get the door AND she called me a fat pig.'

'You get it,' they both shouted back at the same time.

They weren't deceived by what they heard Alice say to me as supposed to what I reported her as actually saying.

'She's the one closest to the door, so she should get it.'

Yes, we argued about everything in our house Alice and I, even the right to open the door.

'Dan, the door,' Dad shouted again.

Though I couldn't see her as she was in another room, I just knew Alice was pulling her tongue at me. Such statement from Dad was born for Alice, moments such as these. I sighed heavily for everyone to hear how discontented I was at actually making the effort to get to the door; it was a last ditch attempt which everyone, everyone ignored! As I went for the door, I wondered why I was born into a lazy household and equally why it had to be me all the time, me or no one else, urgh!

I dumped my sports bag I had slung across my shoulder to the floor making sure it made a very annoying thudding sound and also that it was placed conveniently at the bottom of the staircase where Alice was at a high risk of tripping over it and doing the most damage. Mission accomplished, I then trudged to the front door as if I was wearing lead boots. I hoped that by now the person would have gone away before I got there. I could see a silhouette of the person through the glazed glass suggesting that my plan was failing. I opened the door with lacklustre interest, I hadn't given up trying!

'Good Day, mate. Is this number 85?'

I nodded then froze almost instantly.

'I'm looking for Daniel Chambers. My name is…'

I recognised the voice. At that point I looked up then rudely left the stranger at the doorway as I screamed back into the house like I was fleeing from a fire.

'Dad, Mum! Mum, Dad!'

I was struggling to get the words out of my mouth. I was speaking that weird language again.

'You are not going to believe this!'

My head was now clear as was my thoughts.

'Calm down.'

'What is it; you look like you've seen a ghost?'

'There's only Max Dillon stood at the door.'

'Max who?' said Mum.

'Max Dillon, who's he?' Alice enquired lazily.

'Max Dillon only happens to be the lead singer of The Slimes.'

'And he's here at our doorstep? Don't be silly,' said Alice.

'I'm not being silly, I'm serious.'

'I thought you said the Slimes are on tour in the States.'

'Besides, what would he be doing stood at our doorstep anyway. You must be imagining things again.'

'Yeah they supposed to be on tour but…I know but, but, I'm not imagining anything.'

Maybe Mum and Dad were right; I threw Alice in the frame, too. I must be seeing things. How stupid of me to have thought that Max Dillon, the heartthrob of millions of teenagers the world over was stood at OUR door. I would go back to where I had left the main door wide open, shut it and think nothing of what I saw, at least what I thought I saw. There was only one slight problem; I couldn't shut the door because Max Dillon had occupied the doorway with his huge body frame!

'There you are. You ran off so fast, I couldn't catch if you said you were Dan Chambers or not, are you Dan Chambers?'

To Max Dillon's surprise, I prodded him to make sure he was real then ran back in again.

'Dad, Mum, you really have to come and see this AND no I'm not imagining things.'

I dragged Dad and Mum awkwardly to the front door as quickly as I could. I had this horrible feeling that before we got there Max would have either turned into an Alien or evaporated into thin air, luckily he did neither!

'Dad, Mum, look that's Max Dillon.' I pointed at him.

'Good day Phil, Susan Chambers. How you doing guys?'

He spoke in his trademark Australian accent.

'Hang on, how does he know...are you secret fans...what's going on here?' I said totally baffled.

'Okay, Dan, I did get a special request from certain people to come and say hello to UK's biggest Slime fan.'

The certain people he was referring to most definitely would be Mum, Dad and the Mayor.

Wow! There I was stood still like a statue not sure what to make of this very surreal situation. I didn't know whether to pinch myself or pinch Max to make sure it wasn't a dream and that it really was happening. As if I needed a second confirmation.

'Check this out, Dan.'

Max fumbled in his shirt pocket and produced a neat brown envelope which he handed over to me.

'Concert tickets for me!'

I quivered as I spoke.

'Not quite, these are tickets for you, your entire family and a friend of your choice to attend our World concert tour coming up later in the year in any UK City of your choice and here's the deal, all expenses paid.'

'Wow!'

'Front row tickets.'

'Wow!'

'Plus you will get to meet with me and the rest of the gang back stage at the end of the gig.'

'Wow!'

*Wow!* That's all I kept saying, that's all I could say, no other words could come out of my ecstatic mouth.

'Talking about the rest of the gang, the surprise, it doesn't end there you know.'

'What, there's more?'

'Well you didn't think I'd come alone did you?'

'You mean...'

Max turned and improvised the sound of a whistle using his fingers and mouth. It was so deafening he nearly took my head off, but I didn't mind!

'Come on in guys, the party's right here.'

'Wow, you mean you brought the whole band with you?'

'Well I can't sing and play our latest hits to you all alone now can I.'

Sure enough the rest of the sensational Slime band started to waltz into my house. The other vocalists, the bass guitarist, the keyboard player Kris, the drummer Kray Zee, they were all here. This was too much for me to bear; I genuinely did not know what to say.

'You want to play here?'

'If it's okay with you that is? You do have a garden big enough don't you?'

I nodded slowly as if I was in a trance, I so needed a slap from someone to wake me up, where was Alice when you needed her! So that Saturday I along with my neighbours and many, many more, we were treated to a live concert of the best rock band ever right there in my garden. Blistering conditions! What blistering conditions, I didn't feel a thing!

We are the Slime
We're going home to you
We are the Slime
What ya gonna do
Sing it from the rooftops
Sing it on the streets
Sing it in the bathroom
Sing it when you eat
Drum it in their ear holes
Drum it to your friends
Sing it to your Parents
May it never end?
Slime! Slime! Slime!

We are the Slime
We're dangerously cool
We are the Slime
What ya gonna do
Sing it on your holidays
Sing it when you're down
Sing it when you're happy
Sing it when you frown
Drum it in their ear holes
Drum it to your friends
Sing it to your Parents
May it never end?

Slime! Slime! Slime!

We are the Slime
We definitely rule
We are the Slime
What ya gonna do
Sing it to the old ones
Sing it to the young
Sing it to the wise ones
Sing it to the dumb
Drum it in their ear holes
Drum it to your friends
Sing it to your Parents
May it never end?
Slime! Slime! Slime!

Well, all's well they say that ends well.

For all our effort, we didn't get to win the scientist of the year award for the simple reason that we didn't get round to submitting our entry. What with all the photo shoots, interviews, we just couldn't create the time! At the end of the day was it worth the sacrifice! One could argue, we won the best prize of all! I got treated to a live performance of the Slime in the comfort of my own home. Even the mighty Father Christmas could not top that and Alice got Bessie back (somewhat). Our little town was finally on the 'map' and its people had us mere kids to thank for that. Yeah, I would say it was worth the sacrifice. But on a humble note, there really was only one true hero, Alice and who would have thought it eh! So there you go, a true hero or should I say shero! To my parents then, well I take back everything I said about them. It took me a long while to realise it, but I have the best parents in the whole world and won't change them... for anything! And as for me and my sister Alice...everything changed for the better...

'There you are.'

'What?!'

'So where's my new wonder doll?'

'How should I know?'

'Only you do.'

'Don't.'

'Do.'

'Don't.'

'Mum, Dad, Dan's got my new doll Bopsie and won't tell me where he put her.'

'I don't.'

'You do.'

'Don't.'

'Do.'

...well almost anyway.


## The End


I dedicate the writing of this book to Dad's dictionary from which I was able to include several big words!